Brigitta of the White Forest

Brigitta of the White Forest

Book One in the
Faerie Tales from the White Forest Series

Danika Dinsmore

en theos press ❖ Seattle, Washington

First paperbound edition.

ISBN 10: 0-9754042-9-6
ISBN 13: 978-0-9754042-9-4
LCCN: 2010942777

Cover art: Julie Fain
Copyright © 2011 Julie Fain
http://juliefainart.com/

Chapter heading art: Larry Ho
Copyright © 2011 Larry Ho

Cover design: Tod McCoy
Book design: Tod McCoy

en theos press
1122 E Pike St. #1451
Seattle, WA 98122
www.entheospress.com

This is a work of fiction. Names, characters, places, and incidents are either the products
of the author's imagination or are used fictitiously. Any resemblance to actual events,
locales, situations, faeries, or persons, living or dead, is purely coincidental.

Printed in the United States of America.

Distributed by Emerald Book Company.
For ordering information or special discounts for bulk purchases, please contact:

Emerald Book Company
PO Box 91869
Austin, TX 78709
512.891.6100

To find out more about the 1000 Fan Campaign, visit www.thewhiteforest.com.

For my father, Stanley Dinsmore,
who introduced me to my first imaginary worlds
(1929 – 2006)

Acknowledgments

This book has had more incarnations than I can count. Every step of the way I was encouraged and supported personally and professionally. I think of each person below as part of my extended White Forest family, as part of my wonderful, magical imaginary world.

Loving thanks go to my husband Ken for his patience and for handling my creative mood swings. Many grateful thanks to my screenwriting agent Doreen Holmes who first recognized the possibilities of the White Forest. To Bret Brubaker and David Ford for always believing in me and always believing in faeries. Thanks to my fabulous friend and publisher Tod McCoy for taking on this experiment. To Larry Ho, artist and moral support system, for his balance of positive vibes and firmness. Good times to my special llama lady Ami Catriona. A million hurrahs for my zealous copy editor Gwendolyn Alley and her son Reed, who listened to the entire book twice. For tiger Erin Mogul and her son Matthew for being two of my first readers. Big smiley thanks for spiritual support from Rev. Angelica Taggart. Hugs for late night laughs and weekend faerie mischief on the Sunshine Coast with Angie and Craig. Super thanks for invaluable critiques and encouragement from fellow writer Sara Nickerson. To all the cheerleading members of SCBWI and Indie Debut. Sincere gratitude to Andy Smallman of Puget Sound Community School and students Ella Shaw, Emma Kahn, and Ivaly Cline for being my official test readers. And lots of warm fuzzies to my mom, Dale Dinsmore, who always told me to do what I love and the rest will follow.

Chapter One

Brigitta leaned out the window of Auntie Ferna's cottage and balanced on her stomach in the sill. She spread her arms wide open and slowly lifted her legs. Her balance shifted forward and she dove, head first, out the window.

She somersaulted through the air and caught herself just above the large rock burrowed partway up Fernatta's ancient tree. She fluttered the rest of the way down to the rock and looked back up at the window.

Not bad, she thought.

She turned and sat down, facing north, so that the entire village-nest of Gyllenhale was spread before her. She tucked the loose strands of her dark auburn hair back into her hair bands and settled into a patch of moss, listening to the children's voices drifting out the window. Brigitta's little sister Himalette shrieked from somewhere inside the cottage and Brigitta cringed.

"All eyes up front!" called Auntie Ferna from inside and the voices quieted. "Today's lesson will be on the history of the Festival of the Elements."

Brigitta groaned and pulled her knees to her chin. She narrowed her olive eyes and watched the flow of faeries zipping in and out of the busy marketplace below.

Several high-pitched squeals pierced the air and Brigitta turned her attention toward the sound. Two male Elder Apprentices from the Center Realm hovered at the top of a very tall tree. Suddenly, they dropped, free-falling until they caught themselves in the air directly in front of the excited faces of three Water Faerie girls sitting on a long branch at the bottom of the tree. Brigitta recognized them; they were from Rioscrea, the village-nest southeast of her own home. The girls applauded and squealed some more as the two boys took a few bows.

"Big deal," muttered Brigitta.

Sliding from the branch, the girls took to the air, playfully circling each other as they made their way through the trees. Brigitta caught sight of the shiny new markings at the ends of their wings.

"They've been changed!" she gasped.

She glanced over her shoulder at her own dull green and yellow wings, then back at the young faeries who disappeared into the busy marketplace.

Brigitta leapt from the rock and flew down past Fernatta's garden arranged like an enormous leafy welcome mat in front of her tree. She glided over the path that led down through the village-nest and descended to Spring River. She landed on the shore at the edge of the marketplace, which was alive with dancing and singing and shouting and laughing under a hundred woven tents pitched on both sides of the river. Dozens of Water Gardeners bobbed in their reed boats, flitting their wings and calling out the names of their crops. *Sharmock! Gundlebean! Dragon flower!*

Brigitta took a deep breath and entered.

Busy stalls crammed the riverbank where Water Faeries offered weather spell ingredients, Fire Faeries displayed feather paints, Air Faeries bartered with bolts of cloth, and Earth Faeries spun delicate candle webs. Brigitta caught a whiff of baking pipberries and her stomach growled in response.

She spotted the three girls as they passed the pink and green tingermint tent, their fresh destiny markings taunting her as she buzzed along behind them. Tilan, the eldest, proudly sported wings marked with a blue moon and three silver shooting stars, the symbols for a Star Teller.

"That wouldn't be so bad, staring up at the sky each night," thought Brigitta as she dodged a family of burly Earth Faeries.

Tilan and her two friends stopped at a tent where a wispy Air Faerie woman was weaving white lyllium flowers into a basket. Brigitta landed behind them, stumbled on a tent peg, and knocked into the weaver. The girls laughed as Brigitta apologized to the Air Faerie.

"Brigitta of Tiragarrow!" said Kyllia, a radiant golden-hued faerie whose wings bore the markings of a Village-Nest Caretaker.

"Running errands for your momma and poppa?" asked Tilan.

"No . . . I . . . " Brigitta stepped back and tucked in her immature wings.

"Where's Himalette? You're not babysitting today?" Tilan looked around the marketplace.

"No . . . well . . . "

"Why don't you come with us then?" teased Dinnae, pink and plump with a wide smile. She leaned closer.

"We're going to the Center Realm to watch the festival preparations." She fluttered her rosy wings, freshly colored with an inner eye glyph and two radiating lines at the tip of each.

"You've got your destiny markings," said Brigitta, pointing at Dinnae's wings.

"Well, nothing gets past you, does it?" said Dinnae. "You must get your smarts from your poppa."

The other two burst out laughing.

The two male Center Realm faeries emerged from the crowd and presented Tilan, Kyllia, and Dinnae with yellow flutterscarves. Brigitta stood quietly as they all turned to leave.

"Aren't you coming along?" asked Tilan, waving her new flutterscarf.

Brigitta wondered how many gundlebeans her momma would ask her to shell if she ditched Himalette in Gyllenhale. "Sure, I'll . . . first . . . I have to . . . " Brigitta motioned vaguely behind her.

"Get permission from your Auntie?" suggested Dinnae.

The three girls batted their eyelashes at Brigitta, who said nothing.

"Come on, let's go," said one of the Elder Apprentices.

They left Brigitta standing there without a good-bye, laughter trailing after them like their scarves.

Brigitta landed on Fernatta's porch and entered the cottage. She could hear her Auntie in the gathering room, deep into her lesson.

"Auntie, I was just wondering—" began Brigitta as she stepped into the room.

"Do not interrupt, child." Fernatta glanced up from her Chronicler's book, her silvery hair dancing like fire.

Sitting on the floor in front of her, a dozen large-eyed faerie boys and girls burst into giggles. Himalette sat in the front row playfully shaking her finger at her older sister. Brigitta glared at her.

"Yes, Auntie." Brigitta slid down to the floor.

Fernatta turned back to her students. Although all teachers in the White Forest were called Auntie and Uncle, Auntie Ferna really was Brigitta's Auntie. She was her Great Auntie, her poppa's mother's sister, and Brigitta often flew between their two village-nests trading objects back and forth for them. She didn't mind flying errands so much, as long as her momma didn't make her drag Himalette along with her.

Like every other teacher in the White Forest, the ends of Fernatta's wings were marked with two circles, one inside the other, resembling the two moons or the inner part of an eye, and two radiating lines. The direction of the radiating lines, downwards toward water and earth, meant she was a Chronicler, and was in charge of teaching the children faerie lore and history.

"It is important to remember," Fernatta addressed the children, "that the Festival of Elements is not all fun and games. Our forest depends upon the magic of the festival. The exact combination of elements protects the forest from the beasts who would love access to our home.

"As long as the Elders balance the elements at the end of each growing season, the forest is protected," Fernatta continued. Brigitta mouthed the rest of the familiar words as Fernatta spoke them aloud, "And those nasty beasts can only dream of getting inside."

Folding her arms over her knees, she sighed and stared at a patch of light streaming in through the window. She pictured Dinnae's new destiny markings: inner eye circles with lines radiating toward fire and earth. So, she was to become a Cooking Teacher, thought Brigitta. How terribly dull.

A fluttery shadow appeared and danced in the light. Another shadow joined it and Brigitta watched as the two shadowflies flitted around each other. Up and down and around, the shadows made their way across the floor and onto a set of old books in a bookshelf made of interlocking tree branches.

The shadows danced a moment more, then disappeared from the light. Brigitta stared at the spines of the books on the bottom shelf. She turned her head sideways so she could read the titles: *Faerie Lore & Lineage . . . Songs & Dances . . . Potions & Recipes . . . Maps & Passages . . .*

Brigitta glanced up at Auntie Ferna, still absorbed in her lesson, then slipped *Maps & Passages* from the shelf and opened the book. The first page contained a map of the entire White Forest. The Earth Realm was spread across the top, the Air Realm to the east, the Fire Realm to the south, and the Water Realm in the west.

She flipped through the pages. There were detailed maps of each village-nest, starting with the Earth Realm:

Dmvyle, Grobjahar, Ithcommon, Gyllenhale . . . She flipped past them all until she got to her home, the village-nest of Tiragarrow in the Water Realm.

A blue line marking Spring River flowed east of Tiragarrow. She followed the line down to where Spring River ended at Precipice Falls and the water tumbled down into a series of underground caverns running the length of the White Forest. Dozens of dotted lines spread out from the falls across the page. She traced the dotted lines with her finger, then stopped. The dotted blue lines . . . the underground caverns . . . someone had mapped them! Someone, at some point in time, had explored the caverns and drawn up this map.

She turned back through the pages and took a closer look at each one. There were dotted lines running through every single village-nest. Some branched off of others, and some seemed to start and stop at random. She wondered who had mapped them all and how come she had never heard anyone mention it before. All faerie children were told the caverns were water channels that kept the forest lush and fertile. She hadn't even considered that it was possible to explore them.

Auntie Ferna's voice cut into Brigitta's thoughts: "The Great Hourglass of Protection was a gift from the Ancient Ones when they brought us north to this land long ago. It sits in the Center Realm where the High Priestess and Council of Elders preside."

The Center Realm! Brigitta searched through the book until she came to a map of the Center Realm. In the middle of the page, the Hourglass of Protection was labeled in dark silver. Off to the side, a dotted line led from the drawing of a tree stump into the Elder Chambers, fondly referred to as The Hive.

She looked up from the book. Who else knows about this passage, she wondered, staring out over the heads of the young faeries. Turning back to the map, she re-examined the dotted lines. Then, with her heart pounding in her chest, Brigitta carefully and quietly began to rip the page out of the ancient text.

"Ever since the Great World Cry many seasons ago, Faweh, the world outside the White Forest, has been in complete elemental chaos."

Fernatta paused and Brigitta's fingers froze in mid-tear. She peered up at her Auntie, who was leaning in close to her huddled students. "There exist dangerous beasts with hideous hearts and haphazard magic. No place for faeries."

Brigitta gave one last quick tug and the page came loose. She folded it twice and tucked it into her tunic pocket.

"This is why we must set the Hourglass of Protection just right every season-cycle, so that our forest remains protected. Brigitta?"

Brigitta whipped her head up and slammed the book shut. "Yes, Auntie!"

"You had a question?"

"Uh . . ."

The faerie children laughed as Fernatta studied her great niece. Her mouth was stern, but her eyes twinkled. She removed a small turquoise keronium glass from the shelf.

"I have something for your poppa." She handed the glass to Brigitta, who got up off the floor and took the fragile object from her Auntie. "Be careful with it. This one had to be melted down and reblown four times to get it right."

Brigitta imagined being shut inside a furnace room for many moons and shivered at the idea of being destiny-marked as a Keronium Glass-Blower.

"Why don't you take it to him? I'll bring Himalette home after her lesson." Fernatta winked at Brigitta.

"Of course!" Brigitta called, sailing out the door.

Chapter Two

$\mathcal{B}$rigitta sped through the forest to the Center Realm. She dodged the festival organizers and headed to the top of the Water Faerie grandstand. Dozens of faeries erected booths outside the immense festival grounds, preparing them for displays of arts and crafts and inventions. She scanned the booths and then turned her attention inside the festival grounds. In three suns time, every faerie in the White Forest would be gathered in the grandstands to watch the resetting of the Hourglass.

The grandstands were divided into four sections, one for each elemental realm, forming a "U" around a large silver oval platform. Five ornate wooden seats were positioned in front of the platform for the Elders and High Priestess. Suspended above the platform was the gigantic Hourglass of Protection, held in place by a twisted mass of tree branches emerging from two enormous uul trees on either side of the festival grounds.

Brigitta spotted Tilan, Kyllia, and Dinnae at the top of the Air Faerie grandstand, peering over the backside. She flew over and landed next to them.

"Well, look who's here!" said Tilan in mock amazement.

"Where are the boys?" asked Brigitta.

"They had important work," said Dinnae. "They are Elder Apprentices, after all."

"And it's only three suns until the festival," Kyllia pointed out.

They turned to watch four faeries hauling decorations out of a carved trunk. Brigitta examined Kyllia's wings. Two deep green wisps adorned the ends.

"Are you sure you want to be a Village-Nest Caretaker?" Brigitta finally asked.

"It's my Life Task," Kyllia said, shrugging her shoulders. "Ooh, look!" She pointed as the decorators began to string shadowfly lanterns in the trees.

"But it's just one thing. What if you stop liking to do it? What if . . . ?" Brigitta couldn't think of a single thing she liked enough to do for the rest of her seasons.

A dark-haired sprite zipped past, disturbing Brigitta's thoughts as it narrowly missed her head with the large seed pod it was carrying. Brigitta steadied herself and watched as the sprite dashed off like a mad thunder-bug toward the uul trees.

"Did you see that?" she asked, pointing toward the unapologetic sprite.

The three girls looked up at Brigitta.

"That sprite. It nearly knocked me over with a— with a—big ugly seed pod!"

The girls stared at her blankly.

"Oh Brigitta," sighed Tilan, "who cares about *fringe faeries* at a time like this?"

"I know you're probably a little jealous of our new wing markings and have to make up stories for attention."

Dinnae patted Brigitta's arm as if she were a child.

Brigitta fumed. "I'm not jealous. It's just that—Look, it makes complete sense that my poppa has the markings of an Inventor and my momma has the markings of a Feast Master. They like those things. They're *good* at those things."

"Oh, right. The only thing Brigitta's good at is daydreaming," said Tilan, winking at the other girls.

"I've never heard of destiny markings for a Day Dreamer," Kyllia teased.

"Maybe she'll be the first!" Dinnae chimed in.

This sent the three faeries into fits of laughter. Brigitta's ears began to burn.

"I'm good at plenty of things . . . " Brigitta grumbled. She felt the folded piece of paper in her pocket. "I'm good at . . . I'm good at . . . reading maps!"

"What's that got to do with anything?" asked Tilan.

"Follow me and I'll show you," said Brigitta.

⁂

"Are we done playing around in the brush?" asked Dinnae, examining her hands. She wiped them on a leaf. "Let's go to the river and lie on the sundreaming rocks."

Brigitta and the others were searching through the trees behind the Fire Faerie grandstand. Brigitta gripped the map in her pocket as if that would magically lead them to the hidden entrance.

"Yes, let's," agreed Tilan. "I've had enough treasure hunting."

"Here it is!" Brigitta shouted and fluttered her wings.

She pointed to an old tree stump, covered in vines. She dropped down and pulled the vines away to reveal a large hole at the base. The others drew in around her. Brigitta poked her head inside and felt a cool breeze. "This way."

The entrance was tight. They had to crawl through one at a time until it opened up into an underground passageway carved into the earth. Her friends stumbled and giggled in the dark.

"Shhhhh!" Brigitta hushed them.

The girls pushed each other along and after several twists in the passageway they saw a dim light streaming in from the stone wall. They gathered around and peered through the gap.

On the other side of the wall was an entryway and past the entryway was a chamber. On the far side of the chamber, illuminated by dozens of long silver candles, High Priestess Ondelle of Grioth was leading the Elders through their spell rehearsals. Ondelle stood tall on her dark frame. Her fiery red wings quivered. Both were marked with a large golden eye and four golden lines radiating in four directions, the destiny markings of a High Priestess.

Each Elder held a miniature hourglass in one hand and a yellow keronium glass in the other. One at a time, Ondelle faced the Elders and waved her hands over the objects. Brigitta held her breath, mesmerized by Ondelle's long slender fingers dancing so effortlessly, as if supported by the air itself. Ondelle's deep black eyes glimmered in the candlelight. She turned and pulled her scepter down from a nook in the wall.

Brigitta moved closer to the gap as the Elders

gathered around Ondelle and raised their arms. Ondelle turned around in a circle, pointing her scepter toward the Elders.

"By the authority of the Eternal Dragon, by the wisdom of the Ancients, by the power of faerie Blue Spell— we charge these sands."

"You'd think they'd be sick of practicing by now, they've been at it for moons," whispered Dinnae.

"They have to get it right. They have to practice because of Hrathgar," Brigitta whispered. "A long time ago she tried to steal the power of the Hourglass and was banished from the White Forest."

"Everyone knows that," said Kyllia.

The Elders and Ondelle all closed their eyes and began to chant. Brigitta could feel the reverberations of their voices inside her body. Losing herself in the rhythm of the words, she leaned toward the Elders.

"Brigitta, move back, we can't see," shot Dinnae, tugging on Brigitta's pack.

Ondelle suddenly stopped chanting and opened her eyes. She stared across the room to where the four faerie girls were hiding. Brigitta's three friends gasped and leapt to their feet, but Brigitta was frozen in place by Ondelle's black moon eyes. They grew wide and her face stiffened.

"Come on!" Tilan pulled Brigitta up by her pack straps.

The others fled down the passageway and Brigitta followed. As they emerged from the tree stump, the girls squealed with the delight that mischief brings. Brigitta pretended to laugh with them, looking back over her

shoulder, expecting at any moment for Ondelle to come
flying out after them.

Chapter Three

Brigitta left her friends in the Center Realm and flew through the forest until she came to Spring River. She headed south with the river, racing the leaves caught in its current. The trees broke away and she turned west into the lyllium field that bordered the Water Realm. The smell of the flowers comforted her, and she slowed down to touch the tops of their white petals. She plucked one and stared into its dark center, picturing Ondelle's face and her black moon eyes.

She hadn't dared tell the other girls how that stare had penetrated her. They would have laughed and accused her of trying to draw attention to herself. How easily they had dismissed the entire incident, caring more about which boys they would dance with at the festival. But Brigitta couldn't shake the feeling that Ondelle had known it was her behind the wall, and that Ondelle's look had meant something.

Brigitta hovered in the middle of the field and stared across the dreamy whiteness. She thought about flying down to Precipice Falls to see if she could find another secret passageway, but then remembered the delivery she had for her poppa. Instead, she blew a kiss to the lylliums and headed toward Tiragarrow.

● ● ●

Brigitta's cottage was on the southern edge of the village-nest above a moss glade. The trees in back of their cottage were covered in tangled vines on which the girls could swing into the downy green.

She arrived home to find Auntie Ferna and Himalette sitting on the front porch shelling gundlebeans and singing one of Himalette's made-up songs. Brigitta's momma, Pippet of Rioscrea, emerged from the cottage, followed by the aroma of familiar spices used in her famous goldenfew. The fermented gundlebean stew was a festival favorite.

"Just in time," her momma laughed, handing Brigitta a glass of iced frommafin. She handed drinks to Himalette and Fernatta. "Like your poppa," she added, holding up a fourth glass for Mousha as his ruddy face appeared in the doorway.

"So, Mousha of Grobjahar, you haven't disappeared into the ether after all?" Fernatta teased her nephew.

Mousha pouted as he handed a well-worn potion book to Fernatta. "If I'd known you were going to collect your book today . . . "

"You may borrow it back again after the festival," said Fernatta.

"Hey, Poppa, here." Brigitta pulled the turquoise keronium glass from her pack.

Mousha's eyes lit up and he clapped his hands in

approval. He ran back to his cluttered laboratory to search for a proper gift in trade.

Fernatta examined the bright pink liquid in her glass, and then sniffed it. Pippet paused at the door. Her golden hair was swept into a haphazard pile on her round faerie head. Loose curls stuck to her face and the backs of her dusty coral wings.

Fernatta took a slow sip, swirling it around in her mouth before swallowing. "Ahhh!" she exclaimed. "How do you make such a perfect refreshment every time?"

Pippit only smiled as she made her way back to the kitchen, taking Himalette and the shelled gundlebeans with her.

Mousha re-emerged and presented Fernatta with a tiny red spout snake which she accepted with a gracious smile. Brigitta waved good-bye to the snake as Fernatta tucked it into her tunic pocket. She bid them good-bye and swooped off the porch, leaving her signature cloud of crotia flower scent behind. Mousha patted Brigitta's head and retreated to his laboratory with the keronium glass, his little yellow wings tapping together like contemplative fingers.

Brigitta followed him into the lab and sank down into her favorite mushroom chair, watching his round body bounce about the room. His right wing was stubbornly twisted where he had injured it collecting thunder-bugs as a boy. The brown marks on the ends of his wings looked like dot-less question marks.

"Poppa, Ondelle's a deodyte, right?" asked Brigitta.

Mousha held his new keronium glass up to the light. "Magnificent."

"She has two elements, air and fire?" said Brigitta.

"What's that? Oh, yes, two elements. Very rare. Rare indeed." He set the glass down and pulled a jar from the shelf.

"What's it feel like? Is it like having another faerie inside of you?"

"Three glassfuls?" Mousha asked himself. "No, four." He reached into the jar and began to scoop keronium glassfuls of a powder into a large beaker of liquid. The liquid turned deep purple. He gave the beaker a little shake.

Brigitta sighed and got up from the chair. She fluttered to the door. The frame was wrapped with a gundlebean vine on which Mousha strung his thunder-bug symphony during special occasions. Brigitta stroked the leaves of the vine. They resembled enormous green dewdrops. One of them began to vibrate.

"Poppa, are you going to string the symphony?" she asked hopefully, opening the vibrating leaf.

Mousha grumbled from inside the lab and Brigitta looked up as a sad poof of purple smoke fell off the table and landed on the floor. "Bog stench!" he swore.

Brigitta turned back to the vine just as an orange thunder-bug darted up from the opened leaves. It weaved through the air and into Mousha's lab. It flew about his head and he absentmindedly swatted it away as he examined a large vial of smoke-colored liquid.

Brigitta watched, amused, as the bug explored the room. Mousha poured the smoky liquid into a tube of pink liquid. It immediately bubbled over. He lifted the vial up to the light and gave a satisfied nod. The thunder-bug buzzed over and landed on his hand.

"Ahhh!" Mousha shrieked and fumbled the vial, spattering pink liquid across his face and chest. The vial fell to the ground and shattered.

"You . . . you!" he sputtered pink bubbles from his lips. He searched the room for the intruder as it hovered high above his head.

Brigitta put her hand over her mouth to keep from laughing.

Mousha looked up. "Aha!"

He picked up a crystal atomizer and squeezed it at the thunder-bug, missing it entirely. The bug zigzagged around the room as Mousha chased it with his bug stunner, flinging pink spots across every wall. The thunder-bug landed on a shelf above his work table.

Mousha fluttered up to the shelf on his little wings. "I've got you now!"

"Brigitta!" her momma's voice called.

Brigitta turned toward the kitchen. Pippet stood in the doorway with a spoon in one hand and a handful of gundlebeans in the other. Himalette peered out from behind her.

"You know your poppa is working very hard and—"

There was a CRASH from the laboratory. Pippet and Himalette rushed to the door. Pippet tried not to laugh as she caught sight of Mousha, bug stunner in one hand, shelf in the other, pink liquid dripping from his chin. In the window sill, the thunder-bug sat cleaning itself, emitting low drum beats of annoyance.

"I won't be working on anything at all," Mousha said,

frowning at the floor, "until I get this mess cleaned up."

They all looked at the broken shards on the ground.

"Sorry, Poppa," said Brigitta sincerely as Mousha stared weepy eyed at the remains. His yellow wings tapped together.

"Come on, then," said Pippet, rolling up her sleeves, "let's get to work."

They cleaned up the lab, caught the thunderbug, and put it in a jar for Himalette. When they were done, Pippet gave a satisfied nod, and then her face fell. "My stew!"

Pippet and the girls flew to the kitchen, where the fermented gundlebeans blurped away. Pippet took one whiff and shook her head. "Well, this won't do."

"I'll get rid of it for you, Momma," said Brigitta.

"Take Himalette with you," said Pippet as she doused the fire. "I've got a lot of chopping to do."

"My friends don't have to take their little sisters with them everywhere they go!"

"Please, Brigitta, just take your sister and dump the stew." Pippet eyed Brigitta sternly. "No shenanigans and no trips to the Center Realm."

"I could do it faster on my own," said Brigitta.

"That's enough."

Brigitta grumbled to herself as she poked a stick at the dying embers beneath the hot vat. Suddenly inspired, she turned to her sister, "Himmy, make yourself useful. Grab Poppa's bug stunner and his globelight and the vine from the doorway. We're going to fix up his symphony."

* * *

Brigitta and Himalette peered over the northern edge of Tiragarrow. The warm vat of goldenfew sat between them. Together they tipped it and spilled the stewy contents over the side. Himalette squealed as it sloshed over the trees and bushes and onto the ground below. Brigitta crouched down at the edge of the village-nest and Himalette crawled up beside her.

"Maybe they won't come?" she said. "Maybe they don't like goldenfew anymore. Or maybe it's a specially bad batch."

"Shhhh," Brigitta silenced her sister.

Himalette leaned her chin out over the forest. She made soft popping sounds with her lips for a few moments and then rolled over onto her back and stared at the patches of sky through the tree branches. A loud buzz careened past and they both sat up. They watched and listened as hisses came in swarms from the river, sparkles came in flocks from the lyllium field, and buzzes came in bursts from every other direction. A silent formation of tiny shadows flitted through the trees and landed on a stew-covered branch.

"Shadowflies!" Himalette floated up on excited wings.

Brigitta yanked her back down. "We're waiting for the thunder-bugs."

On cue, there was a burst of little clashing beats. Ricocheting off the trunks of the trees, vibrating beasts of all different sizes, shapes, and colors made their way to the steamy mess below. All the other flying, blinking, and zipping beasts abandoned the meal and slipped back into the forest.

Once the thunder-bugs had polished off the stew, they settled into the branches to digest it, emitting a steady stream of drunken hiccups as they lazed and swayed. The faerie sisters leapt off the edge of the village-nest and glided to the ground. Brigitta examined four thunder-bugs wobbling across a branch while Himalette plucked a tiny yellow beast from a leaf and placed it in a jar.

"Only the biggest and loudest ones, Himmy." Brigitta pulled out the atomizer and sprayed a vivid pink bug with an enormous vibrating bottom.

"I'm going to make up a song for the thunderbugs!" declared Himalette. *Thunderbugs, how you twinkle and shine, how you twinkle and shine . . . "*

"Thunderbugs don't twinkle. Or shine." Brigitta sprayed and plucked a drunken thunderbug from a branch and placed it in a jar, doing her best to pretend that Himalette was in another world, one that was so far away she couldn't be heard.

She practiced her favorite ignoring technique, a hum that radiated from the space between her eyes. "Hmmmmmmmmmmmmnnnnnnnnn . . . " she hummed as she continued through the trees, spraying and plucking thunderbugs until she reached the lyllium field. She placed the jars of bugs inside her pack and turned back toward Tiragarrow.

"Himalette?" Brigitta called. Then louder, "Himalette!"

Her voice echoed through the trees.

"Himmy!" she growled.

The faint sound of laughter danced in the air.

Brigitta followed the laughter into the trees until she came across a large fallen log that sounded suspiciously like a giggling young faerie.

"Himalette, come out of there," Brigitta commanded.

"I found a sprite! I found a sprite!" Himalette called back from inside the log.

"Leave it alone."

"She's pretty."

"Don't touch it!" Brigitta climbed into the long, narrow log. She could see Himalette farther down, illuminated by a blue light. Himalette squealed, and then the light vanished.

Brigitta removed her pack and dug out her poppa's globelight. She rubbed the globe a few times to charge it. After it lit up, she made her way through the log, scrunching down as it narrowed. She held the light up to Himalette and gasped. The globelight flickered.

Himalette was blue from her face to her feet. Even her pink wings and blonde hair had blue tints to them. She waved her blue fingers in front of her eyes.

"Aw, Himalette, I told you not to touch it." Brigitta shook her head. "You know sprites are full of stupid tricks."

"She gave me her blue," Himalette said, checking the underside of her arms.

"What do you mean she gave you her blue?"

"She gave me her blue. Then she went up there." Himalette pointed to a hole in the top of the log. Brigitta squinted up at it and saw nothing but forest and sky.

"Come on, twerp. Maybe Poppa can turn you back." Brigitta smirked. "Maybe," she said under her breath. She turned to exit the log.

Himalette pouted and rubbed her shoulder against the rough interior of the log.

"Brigitta, it itches," she whined.

"Serves you right."

Brigitta grabbed Himalette's hand. The warm blue instantly shot from Himalette's hand up Brigitta's arm all the way to her face. She could feel it spreading down her body and legs and finally her toes.

"Oh, great. I should have left you tied to a tree," Brigitta moaned as she pulled Himalette toward the opening of the log.

There was a bright flash from somewhere outside and a loud, low hum. The log trembled; the globelight went out. A moment later everything was dark and still.

"What was that?" asked Himalette, frozen mid-scratch.

"I don't know."

They quietly felt their way through the log. They emerged from the end and peered through the trees. Nothing looked any different, but there was something odd about the forest, something Brigitta couldn't quite place. Out of Water Faerie instinct, they both looked to the sky. The sun was out, there were very few clouds, and Brigitta could feel no storm on the horizon.

"I'm scared," whispered Himalette.

"Shhhhhhh," said Brigitta.

"I want to go home."

"Stay here."

Himalette sat in the mouth of the log, scratching her

itchy blue face, while Brigitta made her way back toward the lyllium field. When she got there, it looked the same as it had before, but something was definitely wrong. After a moment, she realized what it was. The field was too still. There were no buzzing or flying beasts anywhere.

"Not one shadowfly," Brigitta muttered as she looked across the field to the other side. "Not one—"

Himalette's screaming cut the silence and Brigitta raced back to the log to find her sister pressed up against it.

"What?" Brigitta shook Himalette. "What!?!"

Himalette pointed to the ground with a trembling finger.

The sprite lay there, motionless and gray.

Brigitta picked up a stick and poked at the sprite. It didn't budge. Brigitta bent down and touched it, then retracted her blue hand in horror.

"It's turned to stone!" she exclaimed.

Himalette began to cry.

"Stop that!" Brigitta scolded, more harshly than she had intended.

She opened her pack and pulled out one of the jars. Three stone thunderbugs sat inside. It was definitely some sort of sprite trickery, Brigitta tried to convince herself, she'd make a complaint to the Elders. She dropped the jar back into her pack and put it on so that it swung from the front. "Come on, lola, I'll carry you home."

Himalette sniffled as she climbed onto her sister's back and snuggled between her wings. She folded her own wings flat along her backside. As soon as Brigitta was airborne and heading toward Tiragarrow, the image of

Ondelle's face interrupted her thoughts. That expression Ondelle had made, she suddenly realized what it meant. It was the look of someone who had just been warned.

Chapter Four

Himalette's head bobbed up and down as Brigitta wove around the rocks and branches. The eerie stillness followed them. No buzzing. No chirping. No fluttering.

Brigitta stopped and gazed up at their village-nest. No sounds echoed from the trees. "Himmy, I have to put you down, all right?"

Himalette stepped down from her sister's back.

"Stay behind me," Brigitta warned, "and don't touch anything."

They flew up to the edge of the village-nest. It was completely still. No faeries flew in or out of the nest on festival errands. The nearest cottage belonged to Orl and Edl Featherkind. Orl was Tiragarrow's Caretaker and Edl harvested tingermint in neat little rows in front of their home, which resembled a giant yellow squash stuffed inside a tree with a porch bursting outward from the front door.

Edl Featherkind sat near the doorway with a pile of tingermint sprigs in her lap. She wasn't paying attention to the sprigs, however, she was squinting into the forest.

"Edl Featherkind?" Brigitta called. Edl didn't move. Not an eyebrow. Not a wingtwitch.

Brigitta and Himalette crept closer until they noticed a peculiar grayness to Edl's skin. They gasped as they realized she had turned to stone.

They leapt back in fear, knocking into Orl Featherkind who dangled by his foot from a vine, his eyes wide in alarm. They stared as he swung back and forth. The trees creaked above them.

Brigitta reached out to stop him from swinging. The creaking ceased and a moment later, Orl plunged to the ground and landed with a loud crack as his right arm broke off.

Himalette shrieked, piercing the stillness. Brigitta grabbed her and pulled her close.

"Be quiet, Himmy. Shhhh." Brigitta scanned the surrounding trees.

"But you killed him, Briggy, you killed him!" cried Himalette.

"I didn't kill him," Brigitta insisted, feeling sick to her stomach.

"You broke him!"

"I—I didn't—he can be—fixed."

They looked down at Orl Featherkind. He was definitely broken. They looked back up at each other in panic.

"Momma and Poppa!" the sisters cried.

* * *

The young faeries entered their cottage and made their way to the kitchen. Pippet's stone body leaned over her new pot of bubbling goldenfew. Her head was turned toward the window, a startled look upon her face.

"Momma!" Himalette ran toward her mother, but Brigitta yanked her back.

Brigitta nodded in the direction of the broken faerie outside. Himalette stood there shaking and whimpering as Brigitta tip-toed to the counter and picked up a pitcher of water. She leaned over and doused the fire underneath the pot.

"Don't go anywhere," Brigitta whispered. "I need to check on Poppa."

Himalette nodded gravely as Brigitta made her way to Mousha's laboratory. She froze in the doorway.

Mousha was balanced in the window sill on his hands and knees.

Himalette entered behind her, crying into a pillow.

"Shhhhh! Be careful," Brigitta warned. "We have to get Poppa down."

She took a cautious step toward him. Then another, and another. She slowly reached out for his left wing. Himalette drew in her breath. Mousha's balance shifted and he plummeted over the side of the window.

"No!" The girls screamed as they heard his stone body crashing through the branches below.

Brigitta zoomed out the window faster than she'd ever flown before. She dove after Mousha as he fell through the trees. She grabbed a hold of his leg and flapped her wings as hard as she could, but she could barely slow him down. She felt movement above her, and then Himalette was there, grabbing her leg.

As they rapidly approached the ground, they became tangled in the dangling tree vines. The vines wrapped around their legs and bodies and pulled them back, catching their fall just before they hit the ground. They hung there, frozen in disbelief.

Brigitta finally let out her breath. "Can you untangle yourself?"

"I think so," whispered Himalette.

"Be careful."

Himalette unwrapped herself from the vines and fluttered to the earth. She dragged a large clump of moss from the glade and they lowered Mousha onto it.

They dropped down beside him and inspected him from head to toe.

"I think he's okay," Brigitta sighed, "other than..." She glanced over at Himalette, who was stroking their poppa's stone head. Brigitta felt a storm of tears gathering inside of her. She immediately swallowed them and tightened her jaw.

Himalette looked up at her sister. Her cheeks were stained with blue-tinted tears. Brigitta wiped them with her sleeve. "Come on," she coaxed, "we'll go to the Elders. They'll know what to do."

The sun was sinking over the forest by the time Brigitta and Himalette arrived at the Center Realm. They were exhausted and Brigitta was worried about her sister. Himalette had never been so quiet in all her life. Under different circumstances, Brigitta would have been overjoyed by the absence of silly songs and annoying questions.

As soon as Brigitta and Himalette landed, they knew all the faeries in the Center Realm were turned to stone as well. They held each other, trembling, as they passed two faeries frozen in the middle of raising a banner. Another three were assembling booths. Brigitta swiftly herded Himalette away from a faerie whose leg had broken off when it fell to the ground, and past another whose wings lay shattered beneath her. There were frozen faeries in mid-taste of food, showing plans to festival organizers, and sitting in the trees holding decorations. All of the faeries' faces were turned in the direction of the Hourglass.

Brigitta and Himalette made their way past the grandstands and into the arena. They surveyed what looked like a battle scene, or at least what Brigitta imagined a battle scene looked like, as she had never witnessed one. Everywhere she looked there were frightened stone faeries: some in the stands, some on the ground, some hanging in the giant uul trees, some whole, some broken. Himalette gripped Brigitta's hand as they stepped through the arena toward the platform.

They had never been this close to the Hourglass. No one was allowed on the platform without an Elder. They climbed the silver stairs and gazed, dejected, at the figure of Ondelle, their High Priestess. She stood overlooking the festival grounds with a determined expression. Her scepter lay on the platform in front of her. Himalette reached down to pick it up, then stopped herself before Brigitta could scold her. She scratched her blue shoulders as they stared at

Ondelle's stone face. Brigitta could no longer hold her tears. They streamed down her cheeks as she choked on her sobs.

"Briggy?"

Brigitta didn't respond. She wiped her tears away with quivering fingers and did her best to compose herself. She studied Ondelle's eyes, no longer intense pools of black, but hard and gray. Even turned to stone, Brigitta thought she was the most beautiful faerie in the White Forest.

She turned and looked in the direction Ondelle was looking. Every other faerie Brigitta could see was facing the Hourglass, but Ondelle had her back to the Hourglass, and was looking out over her faeries. Brigitta gazed down at the scepter.

She had the look of someone who had just been warned.

She stared back up at Ondelle, willing her eyes to tell her something. What had she been trying to do?

"Priestess Ondelle . . . it's Brigitta . . . of Tiragarrow . . . Please . . . help us."

She reached out and touched Ondelle's hand. The coldness of her fingers shocked Brigitta and she leapt back. Her foot hit the scepter, knocking it from the platform, down the steps, and into the dirt below.

Horrified, Brigitta flew down to retrieve it. Next to the scepter was an open black seed pod, the same kind the rude sprite had been carrying earlier that day.

She picked up the seed pod and examined it. It was surprisingly light, but firm. She knocked on it with her knuckles and turned it over in her hand.

"Hey Briggy, watch!" called Himalette from the platform.

Brigitta placed the seed pod in her pack, retrieved the scepter, and flew back up to the platform. She found Himalette pressed up against the branches that cradled the Hourglass, watching the sands inside fall like a heavy, rainbow-colored rain.

Himalette reached out to touch the glass.

"No!" cried Brigitta.

"It's okay," Himalette insisted and she tapped on the glass. As she did, little blue sparks flew off her finger. "See? It likes me!"

Brigitta pulled Himalette's finger away. "That's enough."

Brigitta turned to survey the scene once more. She went back to Ondelle and carefully placed the scepter in her hand. Then she looked out to the frightened faeries on the festival grounds. "What were they all looking at?"

"Maybe this is where the bright light came from?" Himalette offered, "before everyone became . . . " Her voice trailed off and her eyes filled with tears.

"But the Hourglass protects the White Forest," Brigitta insisted, gazing up at it. The top half was nearly empty. The bottom half held a mountain of multi-colored sands.

"Briggy, what happens when the Hourglass runs out?"

Chapter Five

For the first time in her young life, Brigitta wished she had paid more attention to her Auntie Ferna's lessons. Being able to string a thunder-bug symphony wasn't going to help them now. She didn't know exactly what would happen when the Hourglass ran out since no living faerie knew a time when the Hourglass hadn't protected the forest by keeping the elements balanced and harmful beasts at bay. And even though she couldn't remember the details, she did know that without the Hourglass there would be no White Forest. It was how the Ancients had protected them long ago and how it had been ever since.

Brigitta began to suspect that she and Himalette were the only two unchanged faeries left in the forest. Their spirits sank lower and lower with each stone faerie they passed. Eventually, it dawned on them that all the other beasts were stone as well: the snakes, the birds, the beetles, the grovens. The grovens were especially pitiful, with sad wide stone eyes and clownish stone lips. Himalette patted the top of a groven's head as she passed, then reached down and gave it a careful squeeze. Its bulbous toad-like face didn't respond.

There was only one faerie left in the entire forest who Brigitta thought might be able to help them. This was truly her last hope, and she didn't have much hope at that, but she didn't say this to Himalette as they flew northwest toward Gyllenhale.

When their wings grew weak, they ran. When they could no longer run, they plodded along until Himalette tripped over a root and collapsed into tears. She climbed onto Brigitta's back. With aching arms she held Himalette steady with one hand and the flickering globelight with the other. She hummed along the way to keep them both company.

Himalette was falling asleep by the time they arrived. Brigitta roused her, for she was far too tired to carry Himalette up to Auntie Ferna's cottage. With the last of their energy, they fluttered up to their auntie's porch.

Brigitta handed Himalette the globelight.

"You stay here, lola," Brigitta said, "I'm going to see if Auntie Ferna is home. If she's—"

"Broken?" Himalette asked.

"Just stay here," Brigitta instructed.

"Briggy, how come everyone turned to stone except us?"

"I don't know."

"What are we going to do?" Himalette was too tired to cry.

"We'll stay the night here and decide in the morning."

Brigitta entered the dark cottage and waited for her eyes to adjust. She eased her way toward the kitchen. "Auntie

Ferna?" she called as she picked up a breath-lantern. Brigitta blew into it and a small orange flame appeared inside.

"Auntie Fer—" she stopped herself as she entered the den and spotted Fernatta, who stood immobile over a potion book on a pedestal. She lifted the lantern and craned her neck. It was the same book Fernatta had retrieved from Mousha earlier that day.

She looked up at her Auntie's face as every last bit of hope drained from her body. Fernatta was looking anxiously out the window, no doubt just as surprised as everyone else by the strange and sudden flash of light.

Himalette screamed from outside. Brigitta flew through the cottage smack into Himalette in the doorway.

"I saw something!" Himalette cried. "Something moved in the forest."

"It was just the wind in the trees," Brigitta said.

They both listened. The night was completely still.

"Come inside," Brigitta said, guiding Himalette into the cottage. "Let's see if we can find a way to change our skin back."

Himalette scratched her blue face as she entered. Brigitta glanced out into the trees one last time before closing the door.

* * *

After placing a scarf over Fernatta's head to cover her face, Brigitta set Himalette in front of a warm fire in the den and grabbed the potion book from the pedestal. "Sorry, Auntie," she said.

She looked down and spotted her poppa's tiny red spout snake peering up at her from inside Fernatta's pocket.

"Hey there," cooed Brigitta. She grabbed a small vile and slipped the spout snake into it. She capped the vile and held it up to her face. "You're lucky you're an invention, or I bet you'd be turned to stone, too."

She warmed some gundlebeans and made a pot of tingermint tea. She served up the modest meal in the den. Himalette ate quietly by the fire, scratching her legs between spoonfuls, while Brigitta perched at a high table surrounded by pots and jars. She placed Fernatta's potion book on the table.

"I should have paid more attention to my lessons," moaned Brigitta, searching through the book. She located a color changing potion and hoped it would work. She wasn't sure if it was meant for faeries, but it was the only thing she could find. She didn't understand how Fernatta's book was organized and there weren't many illustrations.

"Dragon Flower dew . . . " Brigitta read the labels off all the jars. "Aha." She grabbed the jar, opened the lid, and sniffed, "Hmmm . . . " She poured a yellow keronium glassful into a bowl.

Himalette picked a stick out of the woodbox and poked at a stone spider on the hearth. "Even the spiders are turned to stone," Himalette sighed.

"Dried sharmock root . . . " Brigitta counted three sand-petals full of the dark orange shrivels and added them to the mix. Then she added a few drops of a dark brown syrup simply labeled *alterings*.

"I wonder if the worms underground are stone,

too?" continued Himalette.

"Mix with licotia nectar . . . " Brigitta poured the various liquids into a large beaker. "Allow bubbles to settle to the bottom . . . "

"And little baby birds inside of eggs."

"Done," Brigitta declared, "I think." She peered suspiciously at the dark mixture, then sniffed it. "Only one way to find out." She retrieved two chalices from the cupboard.

Himalette threw the stick into the fire and crawled over to the stone spider. She tapped it with her finger.

"But he doesn't turn blue, like when I touched you," Himalette murmured. She got up from the floor and smiled. "I made a rhyme."

Brigitta poured the liquid into the two chalices.

Himalette moved to the table and examined the seed pod sitting on top of Brigitta's pack. She grabbed the pod and shook it, then placed it on the table and spun it around.

Brigitta lifted one of the chalices to her lips.

Himalette began to sing. "*He doesn't turn blue, like when I touched you . . .* " She watched the seed pod as it whirled around and around.

Brigitta spat out the mixture and dropped the chalice. "Himalette, that's it!" She slammed her hand down on the seed pod.

Himalette jumped back from the table. "What's it?"

Brigitta ran out of the den and into the gathering room. She rushed to the dusty bookshelf by the window and searched the lower shelf. She retrieved the thick manuscript called *Faerie Lore and Lineage*. She ran back to the den and pulled Himalette to the floor with her.

"A History of the White Forest as Chronicled by Fernatta of Gyllenhale, Eighth Faerie Lorekeeper," read Brigitta. She flipped through the pages until she came to an entry for Blue Spell. She remembered the Elders' spell rehearsals. "By the wisdom of the Ancients, by the power of Blue Spell . . . "

"Blue Spell?" asked Himalette.

"It's the most powerful of all faerie magic." Brigitta showed Himalette a passage in the book.

"What's it say?"

"Blue Spell may only be conjured by the acting High Priest or Priestess upon consensus of the Faerie Elders or by authority of the Ethereals themselves."

"What are consenses?" yawned Himalette as she slid closer to the fire.

"It means they have to agree." Brigitta continued reading aloud. "Faerie Blue Spell is reserved for rebalancing the Hourglass of Protection every season cycle or for rare circumstances when extraordinary force is required. Other than to rebalance the Hourglass, there are only three known occasions in which Blue Spell has been conjured in the past: to move the elemental faeries north during the Great World Cry, to create the Hourglass and its protective field over the White Forest, and to expel Hrathgar of Bobbercurxy to Dead Mountain after she attempted to steal the power from the Hourglass itself." Brigitta looked up from the book and stared into the fire.

Himalette picked up the stone spider and walked it

up Brigitta's leg. "Are you going to turn us back?" she finally asked.

"I don't think I can." Brigitta brushed the spider away.

"But it itches horribly," complained Himalette, scratching around the top of her wings to demonstrate. "I'd rather be turned to stone." She stopped scratching and cradled the spider in her hands.

"Don't say that." Brigitta snapped out of her trance. "Listen, I don't know how she did it, because it says it's for Elders and Ethereals only, but I think it's *because* the sprite gave you her blue that we didn't turn to stone."

"So it was good I touched the sprite!" Himalette said.

Brigitta examined the blue skin of her arms and legs. "We have to find a faerie who knows about Blue Spell. If the sprite figured out how use it, maybe someone else has, too. Then we can use it to turn the Elders back to normal so they can reset the Hourglass." She carefully tore out the pages referring to Blue Spell.

"But everyone else is stone. There aren't any faeries left."

"There's still one left," Brigitta held out the manuscript pages and pointed to the passage she had been reading. Her finger landed on the word *Hrathgar*.

Chapter Six

Troubled by nightmares of what they had witnessed that day and visions of what might lie ahead, Brigitta and Himalette spent a restless night huddled near the fire despite their exhaustion. Brigitta did not feel refreshed the next morning, and certainly not ready for the long journey. But she knew they had no choice. They had to get help.

With a fresh pack of supplies on her back, Brigitta paused on the porch overlooking Fernatta's meticulous garden. She looked down at Himalette and straightened her sister's canteen strap, then put on a determined face and grabbed her hand. She felt a hard object in her palm. Brigitta opened Himalette's hand. It was the stone spider.

"Leave it here," Brigitta instructed.

Himalette pouted and set the spider down on the porch.

A little wobbly from the previous day's travels, Brigitta and Himalette flew from the porch down to the river. Doing her best to ignore the hundreds of faeries scattered about in the grass, in the trees, under the tents, and along the river, Brigitta wondered if stone faeries could drown, but quickly put the thought from her mind. They didn't have time for rescuing stone faeries. The only way to save the forest was to turn the Elders and Ondelle back so they could reset the Hourglass.

They followed the river north to the spring and filled their canteens, then headed northeast out of the Earth Faerie Realm toward The Shift. They flew close to the ground navigating through the trees, passing dozens of stone faeries and other forest beasts. All of the frozen faerie faces were turned in the same direction.

They reached a small pond where three faerie boys had been interrupted in the middle of teasing a groven. Brigitta noticed that even the groven's stone eyes were looking through the woods toward the Center Realm. Further on, they encountered a young faerie couple camped out on a giant mushroom. Then, there were no more faeries.

The forest grew thicker and wilder and darker as they traveled. Brigitta thought about flying up and over the trees, like the Air Faerie Perimeter Guards, but the guards' wings were strong and mature and they were talented flyers. Brigitta and Himalette were likely to get tossed back into the trees by a strong wind and tear their wings.

After a lengthy silence, Himalette landed on the ground and folded her arms across her chest. "I'm hungry," she declared.

"Not yet, Himmy," Brigitta answered, landing near a very old and twisted tree.

"You're going too fast," Himalette complained.

Brigitta flew back to Himalette and knelt in front of her. "Listen, we don't have much time and I can't leave you behind. You're going to have to—"

Himalette wasn't listening. She was staring over Brigitta's shoulder. Brigitta turned to see what had caught her attention.

A stone faun sat on a rock with a wooden flute to his lips. Brigitta and Himalette approached him. If he hadn't been frozen, they could never have gotten so close. Once, many seasons before, Brigitta had spotted three fauns hiding behind some trees watching faerie festival games. This one's eyes were closed in a stone reverie.

"He looks happy," murmured Himalette, doing her best not to pet him.

Brigitta peered through the forest. They were very far from the Center Realm and the Hourglass of Protection. "Didn't see what hit him," she said.

"I've never been this far from home," Himalette observed.

Brigitta looked down at her little sister and wiped a dirt smudge from her blue cheek. She opened her pack and pulled out a slice of sweet pipberry bread.

"Here," she offered, "But that's it until supper. Come on."

◗ ◗ ◗

Eventually, the vines became so dense that the girls could no longer fly without getting tangled in them. They pushed their way through the forest, passing occasional songless stone birds perched in the trees. Brigitta was long past humming and concentrated on a breathing rhythm to keep herself moving.

They were both so focused on putting one foot in front of the other that they were completely startled when the forest ended and they found themselves standing before an immense river of dry earth that stretched around the perimeter of the White Forest as far as their eyes could see. Ahead of them, across the shifting dirt moat, was the rest of the world, beginning with the edge of the Dark Forest.

"The Shift," said Brigitta, holding Himalette back with one arm. They stood listening for a moment. There were no trees or plants or beasts of any kind across the large expanse of land. They could hear nothing but the strange sound of the slowly churning earth.

"Are you sure?" Himalette whispered.

Brigitta nodded and moved forward. There was nothing else it could have been. She had heard it described many times by the Air Faerie Perimeter Guards, but this was more endless and empty than she had ever imagined. There was nothing to protect them, and nowhere to hide.

"Is it safe?" asked Himalette.

Brigitta took a few tentative steps into The Shift. She could feel the dirt moving beneath her, carrying her along on its sluggish journey. She fluttered back to her sister.

"Where's the magic field?" asked Himalette.

"Wait here." Brigitta picked up a small rock and stepped back into The Shift.

There was a light breeze, and a strange scent rode in on it.

"What's that smell?" Himalette called, wrinkling her nose.

"The other side." Brigitta threw the rock as hard as

she could. Half-way across The Shift, it passed through a watery barrier and continued out the other side. It landed with a soft *thud* on the outskirts of the Dark Forest. Brigitta returned to Himalette, who quickly hid her hands behind her back.

"What's that? What have you got?" Brigitta demanded.

"Nothing."

Brigitta reached behind Himalette and grabbed her arm. Himalette opened her hand to reveal a stone bird.

"It's just a bird," admitted Himalette. "It was on the ground. It was lonely."

"Himmy, you have to stop taking everything all the time." Brigitta grabbed the bird from Himalette and contemplated where to put it.

"I'll keep it in my pocket," Himalette pleaded. "You won't even see it." Her frightened face softened Brigitta's heart just a little.

"No more, Himmy." Brigitta handed the bird back to her. "Stay close to me and don't touch anything else. Do you understand?"

Himalette nodded and put the bird back into her pocket.

"Will the magic field let us back in?" asked Himalette.

"Anything originally from the White Forest can get back across," said Brigitta. "Anything that comes from the other side has to be escorted by a Perimeter Guard. Like this."

Brigitta took Himalette's hand and carefully led her over the rough earth river until they were half-way across.

They hesitated in front of the force-field, a little bewildered to be standing still and moving at the same time. Brigitta took a deep breath and walked forward.

She felt streams of coldness, not completely unpleasant, like walking through an invisible waterfall. A moment later, they had passed through to the other side. They shivered and paused to look back at the White Forest. Himalette's free hand went into her pocket.

Brigitta looked down at Himalette, whose face was contorted in horror. "What? What is it?"

Himalette pulled her hand out of her pocket and opened it. Instead of a stone bird, there was a pile of gray dust. She looked up with frightened eyes as the dust fell through her fingers.

Chapter Seven

The girls half flew, half hiked through the thick forest in silence for several moon-beats. Brigitta led the way, holding branches back, pointing at tricky areas of twisted roots or vines. Himalette followed, at first cautiously, then curiously, and then finally with no more dread than exploring the forest around her home.

It wasn't so long ago that the past and future could escape Brigitta's mind. She wished she could be more like Himalette and simply forget to worry. But right now, someone had to keep them focused on their task.

"Is this Faweh?" asked Himalette.

"Of course," Brigitta answered while removing a sticky spider web from her hair. "Everything outside the White Forest is Faweh."

"How big is it?"

"Big."

"How do you know?" Himalette ran to keep up with Brigitta.

"Because . . . because . . . I just do." Brigitta held back a thorny branch for Himalette and pricked her finger as she let it go. She looked down at the trickle of blood on her finger, only mildly surprised to discover that it, too, was tinted blue. She wiped her finger on her tunic. "Don't you listen to Auntie Ferna's lessons?"

"Sometimes," Himalette said, "but other times I just watch the shadowflies outside her window."

Brigitta smirked to herself. She had watched the shadowflies so many times she could sometimes figure out what they were saying. They mostly danced about the weather or where flowers were in bloom.

Once Brigitta spent half a morning interpreting a dance about a patch of ripe pipberries. After their lesson, she and Kyllia had found the bush at the top of a steep bank. They had poked at the ripe red berries, which burst with a "pip" and spilled their sweet juice. The riper the berry was, the redder and fuller with juice, and the bigger the "pip" sound it made.

Brigitta shook her head out of her daydream. It was making her crave her momma's iced frommafin. She thought about her momma's nickname, Pippet, and how she always locked up her pipberry supply to keep Brigitta and Himalette from eating them before she could make her specialty drink.

Brigitta's mouth felt dry. She didn't know if there were any pipberries around, but she wouldn't eat off a pipberry bush in the Dark Forest no matter how thirsty she was. She wasn't taking any chances.

She paused for a moment to concentrate. She wanted to stay heading east, but it was much harder to read the air in the Dark Forest, even though Brigitta had been at the top of her class in sensing directions. The elements were just not as cooperative outside the protected realm. The moisture in the air was heavy and stank of mold.

Himalette moved closer to her sister. "Briggy?"

"Shhhh." Brigitta closed her eyes and visualized separating the water from the air as she had been taught in her Elemental Elements class. It was always a matter of balance. When she could feel the balance, she let the foul Dark Forest water fall away and held the air. East, she thought, and the air began to pull. She could only hope it was pulling in the right direction.

She opened her eyes and resumed pushing her way through the trees. Himalette trotted along behind her.

"Briggy?" Himalette tried again.

"Yes?"

"How come faeries aren't allowed to leave the White Forest?"

"A very, very long time ago," Brigitta began in her best Auntie Ferna impression, turning to point her finger at Himalette. Himalette giggled as Brigitta continued, "There were more faeries than you could possibly imagine. All the elemental faeries lived in beautiful villages surrounding Lake Indago in the Valley of Noe. They were taken care of by the Ethereals—"

"The Ancient Ones?"

"Do not interrupt, young faerie," Brigitta scolded. She picked up a stick and used it like an orchestra baton. "Yes, the Ancient Ones, the oldest and wisest of all faeries. They looked after everybody else."

Brigitta assumed an Auntie Ferna stride while she waved her baton to the beat of her lecture. "In those days,

Faweh was peaceful, and the Five Civilizations of the world were strong. There were four Sages, each representing a civilization and an element, and a fifth Tender of the Elements. This High Sage was an Ancient One, an Ethereal Faerie, and he was very, very wise—"

"Like our poppa!"

Brigitta snapped around and pointed her baton at Himalette who jumped back and laughed. Brigitta turned and launched herself over a moss-ridden log. "The powers of the four elements were housed in Lake Indago, which was the entry point to the Center of the World, from which all Faweh's energy comes. The World Sages would gather at a great palace in the Valley of Noe and the High Sage would call forth the energy from the Center World."

Brigitta sped up her baton rhythm. "One day, the World Sages had a bad argument. The High Sage tried to stop them, but the other Sages turned on him. They didn't see why the Ethereal Faeries got to be Tenders of the Elements. They wanted access to the Center World, too. During their argument, too much magic was cast, and the High Sage was accidentally killed. The World Sages threw his body into Lake Indago and fled to their homelands."

"I don't like this story anymore," said Himalette.

"The balance of the elements was lost. The lake evaporated. In order to protect their faerie kin, the Ancient Ones gathered every grain of balanced sand from the dry lakebed, placed them in an hourglass, and moved it to the far north, where it was safer."

"The Hourglass of Protection!" Himalette interrupted.

"Around the Hourglass, they created the White Forest and moved all the elemental faeries there, where they have been protected for thousands of seasons. And when the last drop of water evaporated from Lake Indago, the Center of the World gave a Great Cry, and out sprung The River That Runs Backwards, which starts from the old lakebed, travels north all the way up the land, and goes back into the earth at Dead Mountain," Brigitta paused, dropping her Auntie Ferna impression and flinging her baton into the trees, "which is where Hrathgar lives."

"But what about the Ancient Ones? What happened to them?"

There was a long silence as Brigitta searched for the best path through the trees. The plants and flowers and buzzing beasts were growing more and more unfamiliar. Everything was engulfed in a gloom. The forest choked on undergrowth. Vines wrapped menacingly around trees like thick spiky snakes. There were no silvery hues in the forest leaves, no sudden fields of lyllium, and no thrumming thunder-bugs. Even a groven stench-bog would have been a welcome sight, thought Brigitta.

"They're gone."

"Oh."

It wasn't entirely true, but Brigitta didn't feel like explaining how the Ethereals could only be felt, not seen, and that they only visited a faerie twice, once at birth to mark her destiny and once at the end of life to disperse her spirit.

Auntie Ferna said that the Ethereals still protected all the elemental faeries, but Brigitta had doubts about that.

Her mind filled with images of frozen faces and broken wings, of Ondelle's cold gray eyes, and of her poppa's stone body lying in the moss.

Brigitta coughed. She was having trouble breathing because the air was so dank. As she slipped past a tree with a leggy orange blob cradled in one of its branches, the blob's two black eyes popped open. She hurried along, although it was difficult to go any faster than they were already going. Her body ached and she was terribly hot. Her immature wings felt inadequate. She had never used them so much in her life, not even during festival games. Himalette struggled to keep up with her.

"How do we get to Hrathgar's?" Himalette ran to Brigitta as a high whining cry pierced the air.

Brigitta glanced over her shoulder. "Auntie's book said go east until you get to The River That Runs Backwards, then follow it straight north to Dead Mountain."

"Which way is east?"

Brigitta stopped and pointed, "East!" she declared before moving on again. "You're a Water Faerie, Himmy, it's time you learned how to interpret the clouds and the air. Being a Water Faerie is good for some things, like sensing direction and weather."

"I like Fire Faeries," said Himalette, ignoring her sister's sharp tone. "I wish I could be a Fire Faerie. They get to dance and play with shimmery things. They get to—Hey, look, a caterpillar!"

Himalette stopped. Caterpillars were one of her favorite crawling beasts. She spent many moon-beats watching the ones outside Tiragarrow spin fuzzy pink cocoons which hung from the tree branches in the Gray Months.

Brigitta tolerated the Gray Months by helping her poppa in his laboratory. After the Gray Months came the Grow Months. The Festival of Elements started on the last day of the Grow Months and continued for two days into the Green Months, Brigitta's favorite season. She wondered if there would be Green Months if the Hourglass wasn't turned. And if there were no Green Months, the caterpillars wouldn't know when to spin their cocoons. And if they didn't spin their cocoons, there would be no butterflies in the Grow Months. And if there were no butterflies, there would be no more caterpillars.

"Leave it alone," Brigitta warned.

"It's just a caterpillar," Himalette mumbled to herself. She paused for a moment, then flew to catch up with Brigitta. "Are Dark Forest caterpillars very noisy?"

"How should I know?"

"Maybe they're like our caterpillars and they're only noisy when they're hungry."

"And maybe they eat little faerie girls who talk too much," Brigitta shot back. Her blue skin itched and she burned all over, especially across her wings.

"I was just—"

"Wait. Listen." Brigitta held up her arm.

There was a rustling sound in the bushes, then a muffled whimper.

Brigitta motioned for Himalette to stay back. She silently fluttered up and over to the shaking bush. She lifted a large leaf. A brown object, almost as tall as Himalette, tumbled from the brush, startling the girls. They flew up to the safety of a near-by tree branch.

The object wriggled around on the ground. Something pushed at it from the inside.

"What is it?" asked Himalette as she yanked on Brigitta's tunic.

"It looks like a big cocoon," answered Brigitta.

"It's not like our cocoons at all!"

"Shhhh!"

"Is it going to hatch?" Himalette whispered.

"I don't know," Brigitta whispered back.

"It's saying something."

They listened for a moment, then dropped to a lower branch and watched the cocoon bouncing and rolling around on the ground. "Hurmmmmmmmmmp!" came its muffled cry.

Brigitta snapped off a long twig and poked at it a few times.

"Heeeerrrrmmmmmmmmp!"

"It's saying 'help,'" Himalette determined. "It wants us to help it."

"Help it what to what? Stand on end?" Brigitta dropped from the tree to the ground and Himalette landed beside her.

Brigitta poked at the cocoon again. It bounced up and down and wriggled some more. She wondered what kind of beast could possibly be inside. She reached out to touch it. The brown strands were sticky. As she pulled her finger back several strands came with it.

"C-c-c-caterpillar . . . " Himalette stammered from

behind Brigitta.

"I said leave it alone, Himmy." Brigitta struggled to break the strands off by winding them around and around her stick. "Bog buggers, this stuff is strong."

"B-B-B-Briggy . . . " Himalette's voice was barely audible.

"What!" Brigitta snapped around.

She had been so distracted she hadn't noticed an immense leafy tunnel in the trees. Staring down at them from the entrance was a gigantic, wrinkled, mossy-colored caterpillar with legs the size of tree branches. Himalette stood frozen in terror as it snarled, flexing the hard pinchers of its mouth. Brigitta's heart dropped to her stomach. She opened her lips to speak, but nothing came out.

"Himmy . . . " she finally managed, "back up slowly. Come to me."

Himalette stood there trembling.

"Himmy," Brigitta called again. She inched toward her sister.

The giant caterpillar stretched up into the air and stood on its hind legs, doubling its height. Its arms flailed and its pinchers gnashed the air.

"Himalette . . . " Brigitta moved closer to her. She could almost touch her right shoulder..

Himalette's hand shook as she reached into her pocket. She pulled it out and opened it. Inside sat a little caterpillar. Brigitta looked from the wee beast to the enormous one flailing above them. Himalette slowly set the tiny caterpillar on a leaf and it crept away.

The giant caterpillar maneuvered toward them.

Brigitta lunged for Himalette and pulled her back by the strap of her canteen. The great beast moved forward again. Brigitta searched for an escape route and noticed that the trees were slightly thinner behind them. She pulled Himalette close and leaned into her ear.

"Listen to me," Brigitta whispered to Himalette. "On the count of three, fly straight up as high as you can. Whatever you do, don't stop, Himmy, okay? Okay?"

Himalette nodded.

"One—two—THREE!"

Brigitta flew straight up, pushing through thick vines and webs, scraping her arms and wings. Branches snapped out of her way as she climbed through the air. When she was out of strength, she landed on a sturdy branch and held onto the trunk of the tree, gasping for breath. She looked back down for Himalette and her heart skipped a beat. She wasn't there.

"Himmy?" she called. "Himmy!"

Himalette was still on the ground, caught in the strands of the cocoon. She tried to fly, but her legs and wings were tangled in the sticky mess.

"Brigitta!" Himalette struggled, tangling herself further, as the giant caterpillar approached. She screamed as the terrifying beast descended.

Brigitta leapt from the branch and plummeted head first toward Himalette. She felt a sudden jolt of pain as a branch tore into her right wing with a sickening ripping sound.

The giant caterpillar lunged after the cocoon and grabbed it in its mouth. It turned back around and crawled off through the trees, its branch-like legs kicking up the earth and ripping vines. Himalette dangled from the cocoon, screaming in terror. She fluttered about trying to get unstuck.

Brigitta darted after them, "No! Let go of her, you stupid worm!"

The caterpillar dove into a tunnel underneath an enormous blood-red tree. Brigitta collapsed at the entrance to the hole, her right wing throbbing.

"Hold on, Himmy!" she gasped into the darkness. She heard the distant sound of scurrying and felt a draught of cold air on her skin. She pulled herself to a sitting position and removed her pack. She dug through it, her hands shaking, trying to locate the globelight.

A very small caterpillar crawled across the ground toward the hole. Brigitta pulled the globelight out of her pack and, in a fit of despair, smashed the caterpillar into the ground.

Chapter Eight

The globelight wasn't working. Brigitta panicked. What if she had broken it with her impulsive behavior? She rubbed it furiously with her hand and it remained unlit.

"Poppa," she cried out, "make it work!" She took a breath, counted to three, and tried again. She exhaled in relief as it started to glow

She rolled the globelight into the tunnel, which curved downward so that Brigitta had to fly to keep up with the light. Her torn wing ached so badly she didn't know how long she could go on. The tunnel floor finally evened out and the globelight stopped rolling. She landed and picked it up, listening for any movement. Brigitta rolled the globelight again and ran after it. She rolled and followed, rolled and followed, venturing deeper and deeper into the tunnel until she came to a division.

Himalette's cries echoed from the dark passageway on the left. Following the sound, Brigitta turned left, then right, then left again. The tunnel opened up into a larger, brighter cavern. At the far end of the cavern, the giant caterpillar stood with its back to Brigitta. She slipped into the room, ducked behind a rock, and hid the globelight in her pack.

59

As her eyes adjusted, she noticed that the brightness in the cave was not stationary, but coming from thousands of tiny shifting lights. Brigitta watched the lights crawling around and realized they weren't lights at all. They were small glowing worms. The little beasts covered the surface of the walls and most of the ceiling, crawling under and over each other, filling the cave with a strange scuttling sound. Several dozen large cocoons were spread about the cave, including the wriggling cocoon she had found in the forest. Beside it, the giant caterpillar was bent over Himalette, her feet struggling beneath it.

Brigitta covered her own mouth to stifle a scream. A moment later the giant caterpillar moved away and Himalette sat there cocooned up to her nose in silky threads. She spied Brigitta and her eyes grew wider. She cried out, but the sound was muffled by the cocoon. Brigitta motioned for Himalette to shush.

The giant caterpillar disappeared through another tunnel. Brigitta crawled over to Himalette and pulled at the cocoon threads, which stuck to her fingers as soon as she touched them.

"Hagspit!" Brigitta swore.

The cocoon next to them began to whine and bounce up and down. Brigitta ignored it and struggled to unstick herself from Himalette. She wiped her hands on her tunic and became stuck to it. Himalette whimpered, her eyes panic-stricken.

Something large scurried through one of the tunnels. Brigitta, Himalette, and the cocoon all froze, listening.

The sound passed and they all continued struggling.

The cocoon bounced its way over to Brigitta.

"Grwwwwwww wrrrrrrmmmms!" its muffled voice cried.

Brigitta managed to loosen the threads around Himalette's mouth. Himalette inhaled deeply.

"It's . . . trying . . . to tell . . . us something," Himalette gasped, nodding toward the cocoon, which bounced up and down a few times.

"Yes, it's telling us to hurry up!" Brigitta took the globelight out of her pack so she could search for something with which to cut the threads. "I have to get you out of this thing, Himmy." She looked back at her injured wing. "I can't drag you through all these tunnels. Not faster than a giant caterpillar."

"Grrrrrrrrrrr wrrrrrrrrms!" insisted the cocoon.

"But what about him?" Himalette cried. "We can't leave him behind!"

"We don't have time!"

"Glrrrrrrrr wrrrrrrrrrrrrrrrms!" the cocoon insisted again.

"Glow worms!" Himalette jiggled up and down along with the cocoon.

"Shhhhh!" Brigitta hissed at Himalette, nodding to the tunnels.

"It's saying glow worms," Himalette whispered.

The cocoon nodded frantically and fell forward.

Brigitta stared at the lights crawling across the cave. She moved to the wall and plucked off the nearest glow worm. Pain shot through in her finger. "Ow!" she yelped and dropped the worm.

She bent down and held the globelight up to it. Its feisty oversized jaws clamped at the air with razor sharp teeth. She carefully picked up the wiggling worm between her finger and thumb and followed along the wall until she came to a pile of half-devoured cocoons. She peered inside one of them. It was infested with glow worms. Whatever had been wrapped up for dinner was long gone.

She moved back over to Himalette and set the glow worm on top of her encased legs. It began to chomp its way through the threads. Himalette squirmed.

"Don't let it eat me," Himalette pleaded.

"I won't," Brigitta assured her. "Just enough to get you out of there."

The cocoon wiggled over to Brigitta and started to whimper.

Brigitta plucked two more glow worms from the walls and placed them on top of the helpful cocoon. The worms began to munch. She gathered two more and dropped them on the cocoon's bottom half. Brigitta turned back to Himalette and placed a few more glow worms on Himalette's front and two on her back.

There was more scurrying through the tunnels as Brigitta pulled the atomizer from her pack.

"Poppa's bug-stunner," Brigitta said. "When they bite through the cocoon, I'll spray them with this."

"How will I know when—OWWWW!" Himalette cried out as one of her wings burst through the loosened threads. A glow worm was clamped onto her wing with its teeth. Brigitta sprayed it with the atomizer and, stunned, it dropped to the ground.

Tears streamed down Himalette's face as her left arm burst through the threads with a glow worm attached. When Brigitta sprayed the little beast, it released its grip and fell from her arm.

"I don't like this!" moaned Himalette. "It hurts! It hurts!"

"Shush!" Brigitta sprayed another glow worm with the atomizer.

Sensing movement behind them, they looked up as the giant caterpillar crawled from the tunnel. Brigitta stood up, guarding Himalette and the cocoon with her wings and arms. The enormous beast reared up and waved its black legs just as two long pale ears burst through the top of the cocoon and flailed around, trying to shake the biting glow worms off. Brigitta sprayed them with the bug stunner and they dropped to the ground.

Himalette's second wing burst through the threads. Brigitta grabbed her sister by the hand and yanked her away just as the giant caterpillar lunged at them, knocking the eared cocoon aside. She towed a screaming Himalette to the top of the cavern, still partially encased in sticky threads. The giant caterpillar roared and they dodged its arms and jaws. Brigitta flew in circles about its head and it twisted itself around after them.

Brigitta heard a ripping sound as two legs burst through the bottom of the cocoon and it jumped to attention. She swooped down and grabbed the cocoon by the ears as the giant caterpillar crashed into the wall of the cave.

Brigitta flew from the cavern and into the tunnels

with Himalette by the hand and the cocoon by the ears. Glow worms dangled in lingering threads illuminating the way. They turned a corner and turned again. It got darker and darker as the glow worms dropped away until they could no longer see.

"The globelight!" said Himalette.

"Too late." Brigitta landed in the dirt.

"Owwwweee—" yelped Himalette. Brigitta clamped her hand over Himalette's mouth and removed the last glow worm from her leg. She tossed it onto the ground and the cocoon stomped on it.

The tunnel went pitch black.

There was scurrying in the distance. Himalette whimpered as Brigitta removed her hand from her sister's face.

"We have to get out of here," said Brigitta.

"This way," said the cocoon. "I hear in dark."

Brigitta, Himalette, and the cocoon emerged from the ground in a completely different part of the forest, with fewer trees. The ones that were there were balder or broken in half. The ground was covered in giant caterpillar tracks and remnants of sticky thread.

Brigitta took several deep breaths, relieved to be out in the open air, even if it was moldy. She was so grateful to be outside that it took her a moment to realize that the cocoon was no longer a cocoon. It was a pale brown hairless creature with the face of a frightened rodent and droopy ears that were as long as Brigitta's arms. It trotted up to a tree and rubbed itself free of the remaining cocoon threads, purring in relief.

"I hate caterpillars," said Himalette, frowning at two tiny beasts inching away from the mouth of the tunnel.

Brigitta pulled Himalette from the dark hole in the ground and spun her around, checking for lingering threads and caterpillar damage. Himalette's wings and legs had some nasty glow worm bites and her skin was torn and bleeding. Brigitta ripped a sleeve off her tunic and wiped the bluish blood away. Satisfied Himalette was in no immediate danger, she turned to the curious creature they had rescued who was using his large ears to brush himself off.

"Who are you?" Brigitta asked.

"I Minq!" he said, thrusting his ears straight out from the sides of his head and taking a bow.

"What are you?" Himalette asked.

"I Minq," he said. "What you?"

"We're faeries, silly," said Himalette.

Minq trotted up to Himalette. On all fours the top of his head came up to her waist. He stroked one of her soft wings with his left ear. She giggled in return. Minq turned to touch Brigitta's wings, but she pulled away. Her right wing was torn near the top and bleeding.

"Wing hurt," he said, frowning. He gestured with his ear. "Come. Be safe."

"We're in a very big hurry," explained Brigitta. "We can't stay."

"Come," he insisted. "Come, come." He took Himalette's hand and pulled.

A deep vibrating growl emerged from the caterpillar tunnel along with a gust of cold air. Himalette gasped and wrapped herself around Brigitta. She studied her sister's wounds and the remaining threads stuck to her filthy tunic. She looked up at the sky. The light was fading.

"Fine," she sighed, "lead the way."

Chapter Nine

Minq led the girls through the forest and before long they came to an ancient wall composed of very tall, thick stones and covered with greenish-purple vines. Minq glanced left, paused, then right. He stretched his ears in both directions.

"What are—" started Brigitta.

Minq hushed her with his right ear and continued to listen with his left. He gave a satisfied nod and pulled up a loose mat of grass. Underneath was a miniature version of one of the large vertical stones. He picked it up and placed it into a hole in the wall like a key. He pushed forward into the wall and a door-shaped section of it gave way. He gestured inside with his ear.

"Inside," he whispered, "quick, quick!"

The girls crept in and Minq closed the door behind them. They were inside a tall circular wall of stones. Along the walls, vines smothered crumbling rock structures. The center of the fortress was bare except for the remains of a campfire, some scraps of forest vegetation, and a small pile of wood.

"What is this place? Did someone used to live here?" asked Brigitta, noting how Minq placed the stone key inside a hole in the ground and covered it with a dried bush.

"We safe here," said Minq, his ears darting about. "We stay night. Rest please. I fix wing."

He reached for Brigitta's injured wing and she pulled away.

"Not so fast." Brigitta eyed Minq. "How do we know you won't eat us during the night?"

"Yeah!" said Himalette.

Minq looked aghast. "Why I eat you?"

"Or trade us to a . . . a . . . " Brigitta started.

"A monster," suggested Himalette. Brigitta nodded in agreement and pulled Himalette close.

"You save life. I yours," offered Minq. "I do what you say always." He bowed deeply to demonstrate his loyalty, glancing up at them with a wide smile that looked more like a grimace.

Himalette smiled back and tugged on Brigitta's tunic. "Can we keep him?"

"We're not going to keep him, Himmy. He's not a bird or a butterfly. He's a—he's—uh—"

"Minq!" he stood up and gestured toward them with his ears. "I yours!"

"See?" Himalette pleaded. "He's ours!"

"Excuse us for a moment. Minq." Brigitta pulled Himalette to the other side of the camp and they huddled up. Brigitta glanced back to make sure Minq wasn't following them. Still smiling like crazy toward them, he moved over to the campfire pit and began clearing out some burnt wood.

"Remember what I said about taking things," Brigitta whispered to Himalette.

"He wants to come with us," Himalette begged.

"He'll slow us down. He can't even fly."

"He can help," Himalette pointed out.

"The only one who can help us now is Hrathgar."

Minq's ears, then the rest of him, appeared at Brigitta's side. "Hrathgar?" he gulped. "You not go Hrathgar?"

"Why?" Brigitta asked.

"If you say go Dead Mountain, I go," he said, ears drooping down to the ground. "You save life. I yours."

Himalette squealed and hugged him. He patted her back with his ears.

"But why we go Hrathgar? Much worse than caterpillar. She only look you, turn you stone." He peered around the campsite as if Hrathgar would magically appear by simply mentioning this fact.

"Turn to stone!" Himalette cried. "Brigitta, she can turn things to stone!" Minq and Himalette shivered at the thought.

"Then maybe she can turn them back," Brigitta said.

* * *

Minq built an impressive fire and the girls moved to the pit and sank to the ground. Brigitta divided up some gundlebeans and all three of them sighed as the warm food hit their bellies. After filling themselves almost to satisfaction, Minq excused himself to gather some medicinal plants from outside the wall. Brigitta picked leaves and cocoon threads from Himalette's blue-tinted hair while they waited for him to return.

Himalette scratched at her arms. "It still itches."

"I know. Try not to think about it," said Brigitta.

"Briggy, what if we can't find Hrathgar? What if she won't help us?"

"Shhhhh." Brigitta kissed Himalette's head. "Don't worry, lola." The same questions plagued Brigitta's mind. Himalette's soft hair and the warmth of the fire comforted her a little, but her head felt woozy and her torn wing ached. She wasn't even sure if she would be able to fly in the morning.

Minq returned with an armful of petals, leaves, roots, and an earful of uul tree sap. He mixed a sticky concoction in a cup over the fire.

"See wing?" He held out his ear to Brigitta.

She turned around and Minq slathered the mixture over the tear. She winced from the sharp sting, but the pain quickly melted into a numbing warmth.

"Does it hurt?" Himalette peered at the salve on Brigitta's wing.

"Only at first. Now it feels kind of tingly."

Minq spread some of the mixture on Himalette's glow worm bites. She squirmed with the first sting, then slowly relaxed. She smiled a sleepy thank you up at Minq.

"This learn from Gola," Minq said. "We go her tomorrow. She Drutan."

"What's that?" asked Himalette.

"Tree-woman. Very old." Minq put the mixture down and began fanning their injuries with his ears.

"She can help us?" Brigitta asked.

"She see."

"Have you ever been to Hrathgar's?" Brigitta asked Minq.

70

"If I go Hrathgar, not be here now. Everyone go Dead Mountain never come back." Minq stopped fanning and wrapped Brigitta's wing with a large soft leaf. "Sleep now. Stay close fire."

Minq trotted over to the pile of extra wood, and from behind it, pulled out some brown furry blankets. He handed them to Brigitta, who took them, wondering what had originally worn the fur. She and Himalette snuggled close on one side of the fire as Minq settled down on the opposite side.

Brigitta whispered into Himalette's ear, "When we reach The River That Runs Backwards, we'll fly north and leave Minq behind."

"But I like him," Himalette whispered back into Brigitta's ear.

"We have to, Himmy. Think about our forest and our momma and poppa." Brigitta squirmed closer to Himalette. "Listen to me. Don't make friends, don't make enemies, and never take anything from anybody unless I say it's okay. Do you hear me?"

"Yeah."

"Himmy?'

"Yes, yes, I hear you. No friends."

"We can't trust anyone, not even him." Brigitta glanced over at Minq on the other side of the fire pit.

Minq shifted his ears and opened one of his eyes. He quickly shut his eye again.

Brigitta held Himalette tightly as they drifted to sleep.

Chapter Ten

The next morning Brigitta and Himalette woke early to find Minq preparing a breakfast porridge of mixed roots and the remaining uul tree sap. Their momma was the best Feast Master in Tiragarrow, perhaps even the whole Water Faerie Realm, so they knew what good porridge tasted like. Minq caught their sour expressions as they took their first bites and then put down their bowls.

"You not like?" he gazed at them sadly.

"It tastes like—" Himalette started.

"It tastes just fine," said Brigitta, quivering her wings at Himalette. "It's just a little hot."

Brigitta knew any breakfast was better than no breakfast. There were few rations in her pack and any lessons she'd had on edible plants did not include Dark Forest flora. She picked up the bowl and gave Himalette a steely glare as she took another spoonful. Himalette pouted and did the same.

Minq removed the leafy bandage from Brigitta's wing and inspected her injury. He patted the herbal goo with his ears.

"Heal good," said Minq with a satisfied nod, "but no

fly today." He returned the bandage to Brigitta's wound and cleaned up around the campsite. "We go now."

●　●　●

They set off into the woods with Minq leading the way over twisted roots, around snapping plants, and under protruding limbs. The forest grew more and more menacing as they traveled. Branches and vines reached out for them as they passed. The girls jumped at every rustle, every throaty growl, and every flying beast that crossed their path. The trees grew thicker and taller, until they could no longer see the sky.

Himalette followed Minq, half walking, half flying, with her arms tucked close to her body. Brigitta picked up the rear, twisting around and walking backwards every time she sensed any movement behind them.

"How come there are no birds in the Dark Forest?" Himalette asked.

"What mean?" returned Minq. "Birds everywhere. They watch now."

Himalette stopped and listened. Brigitta shot her a warning look.

"I'm not touching anything," said Himalette. She stuck her hands in her pockets to demonstrate.

"Good."

"I'm not even looking at anything I might want to touch."

They came to a break in the trees where a small and surprisingly picturesque waterfall dropped into a green pool.

Minq took a right at the pool and continued on. Himalette gave the tranquil scene a longing gaze before turning and following Minq. Removing her pack, Brigitta dropped behind and knelt on the moist bank.

She paused for a moment. There was something strange about the pool. Then she realized that even though water flowed into it from the waterfall, the pool didn't appear to lead anywhere. There were no streams from it heading uphill or downhill. And the waterfall wasn't splashing over any rocks into deep caverns, like at Precipice Falls south of Tiragarrow.

The water was completely clear. The pool's color came from the little feathery green plants dotting the bottom. Brigitta stared at her reflection on the water's surface. A strange blue-faced young faerie with tangled hair stared back. She removed her canteen from her pack and reached down. Minq was suddenly at her side, snatching her hand away just before it touched the surface of the water. She gasped and dropped the canteen.

"Pond vile." Minq picked up Brigitta's canteen and handed it to her. He then picked up a stick and touched the water with it. As soon as it hit the surface, one of the green plants stretched out and seized it, dragging it underwater. The stick shook a bit before another plant grabbed hold of the other end and snapped it in two. The little plants let go of it and the broken pieces floated to the surface.

"Don't touch anything, right?" Himalette said from behind them.

"Right." Brigitta rummaged through her knapsack while Minq peered over her shoulder. She pulled her pack to the side, out of his view, and removed the tiny bottle she had found at Auntie Ferna's. "Poppa's spout snake." She smirked as she uncorked it.

She set the bottle on the bank of the pool and out slithered the miniscule red snake. At the edge of the water, it paused, sniffed with its triple forked tongue, then dove into the water, streaking through the pool faster than she could see and faster than Minq's ears could hear. The pond vile snapped at the snake as it propelled itself out of the water and onto the ground in front of them with a wet thud. It was as long and thick as Brigitta's arm.

Brigitta picked up the snake and gave it a test squeeze. A stream of water shot out from its mouth. She held the snake over her canteen and squeezed snake-water into it. When her canteen was full, she pinched the snake's mouth shut, flung it over her shoulder, and corked her canteen.

Brigitta gestured to Himalette who handed her own canteen over. Himalette clapped as Brigitta squirted water into it, then squealed as Brigitta sprayed her face.

Minq approached and examined the snake. Brigitta offered it to him. He shrugged and opened his mouth. She released a stream of snake-water down his throat.

"Poppa's spout snake took third place in New Creations at last year's festival." Brigitta rolled the snake up from the bottom to squeeze out the remaining drops.

"It was supposed to be a fountain," said Himalette.

"It was supposed to work more than once, too," added Brigitta.

"Now snake broken?" asked Minq.

"Not broken," said Brigitta, "just used."

She gave one last little squirt into her own mouth, then released the snake into the grass. It lay there, not knowing what to do.

"Snake be eaten," Minq warned, "you leave here."

"I doubt it." Brigitta gave it a little nudge and it slithered forward. "It wouldn't taste very good."

They watched as a prickly flower leaned over and sniffed the snake as it passed. The flower turned away in disgust as the squishy red snake disappeared into the forest forever.

●　●　●

Minq and the two young faeries trudged through the trees. Brigitta swore to herself that if she could make things right, she would never complain about the long flight to Auntie Ferna's cottage ever again.

Minq had done a decent job on her injured wing, but the severe tear still pained her with every step. She was frustrated they weren't able to fly and was haunted by the image of sand falling through the Hourglass. They were running out of time.

For a land beast, Minq was surprisingly quick and agile. He would trot ahead and return with news of swampy ground or prickly trees, or simply to encourage them. "Listen! Listen! Hear?" he would say excitedly and then bound off.

"Hear what?" Brigitta and Himalette would call out as he disappeared again.

Far past their usual lunchtime, Brigitta began to

hear a great rushing of water in the distance. The roar grew louder and louder until the trees finally opened up and they found themselves standing near the edge of a steep embankment, confronted by a menacing river. The water was dark brownish-green and moved like a storm, churning and fighting against itself as it flowed uphill. Brigitta could feel its pull, even from a distance. She steadied her feet and grabbed Himalette's shoulder to stop her from getting too close.

Their eyes followed the river's path uphill and the girls gasped as they caught sight of an enormous, rugged dark lump of earth surrounded by a dirty haze. Two-thirds of the way up, twisted into the barren rocks, was a foreboding castle.

"Dead Mountain." Minq pointed toward the castle and shivered. "Hrathgar live there. You sure we go?"

"Our forest depends on it." Brigitta swallowed at the lump that had formed in her throat.

"And our momma and poppa," said Himalette, reaching for Brigitta's arm.

Brigitta broke away and stepped a little closer to the embankment for a better view. The river-wind pulled at her, whipping at her hair and tunic. She was drenched in the heavy mist that the river spat out and sucked back in. She grabbed hold of a tree branch for safety. The forest grew right up to the edge and it was a long drop to the river below.

"Careful," warned Minq, holding her back with an ear, "too close edge!"

She scrambled back and glanced over her shoulder at her bandaged wing. She tested it a few times and winced as a sharp pain shot through to her shoulder. "We'll have to fly over the river to the mountain."

"No good," Minq explained. "Bad river-wind. Take you down. Bones come out there." He pointed to Dead Mountain with his ear. He wrapped his other ear around a trunk, picked up a leaf, stretched out, and dropped the leaf over the embankment. The unsuspecting leaf immediately disappeared, sucked into the river-wind. "Best go Gola. Not far. Stay night. Go mountain tomorrow if still want."

"Gola will help?" Brigitta was skeptical.

"Gola see."

"Will there be food?" Himalette held her stomach as it emitted a gurgle to punctuate her question.

Brigitta looked back up at the castle and back down at the river. She removed her pack, dug out the last piece of squished pipberry bread, and handed it to Himalette.

A tiny yellow light emerged from the forest and floated on the breeze toward them. It bumped up against Himalette's nose. "Hey!" she laughed with her mouth full of bread.

The floating light swirled away from Himalette and bumped into Brigitta's forehead. It was fuzzy, as if spun from soft web. It made a hissing noise as it bombarded her face.

"Minq, you don't understand." Brigitta swatted at the light. "The Hourglass of Protection runs out when tomorrow ends. It's supposed to be turned by the Elders or else . . . or else . . . " Brigitta didn't have time to explain. "We have to get to Hrathgar's *today*."

"No time. No time before dark," he insisted. "Come. Gola see."

Himalette held up her hand to the yellow light, letting it dance on her fingers. She grabbed at it as it drifted away, caught in the river-wind.

"It's whispering to me!" Himalette exclaimed as the yellow light picked up speed and spun toward the river.

"Sorry, Minq." Brigitta was adamant. "We really have to leave you now. Thank you very much for all your help. I release you of . . . of . . . I mean . . . you don't have to be ours.

"Come on, Himmy." Brigitta slung her pack over one shoulder and turned to retrieve her little sister. "Himalette!"

Himalette was dangerously close to the embankment. She stood there, blue-tinted hair and dirty tunic whipping wildly as the yellow light flew over the edge and was sucked out of sight.

Himalette pouted. As she turned back toward Brigitta, the ground beneath her gave way. She screamed as she slipped and the river-wind pulled her down toward the mad water. She beat her little wings against the wind and grabbed hold of a long tree root. Her legs flailed behind her as she struggled, unable to fly out of the current.

"Hold on!" cried Brigitta.

Minq wrapped his forearms around a tree, braced his legs against two sturdy roots, and held his right ear out to Brigitta. She took hold of it, surprised by its strength as it wrapped itself around her wrist. She inched her way out until she could almost touch Himalette.

"Grab my hand!" commanded Brigitta.

"I can't!" cried Himalette. "I can't reach it!"

"Yes, you can." Brigitta slid a little more toward

Himalette and stretched downwards. Her pack slipped from her shoulder and down her arm. The ground moved beneath them and the river-wind pulled as if the world had opened up and was trying to swallow them. Brigitta reached for her pack a second too late. It slipped off her arm, dropped to the ground, and disappeared over the embankment.

Brigitta stretched out and grabbed her sister. She held on as Minq pulled them out of danger. They collapsed under the tree and caught their breaths. After her heart had stopped racing, Brigitta smacked at the leaves above her. "I can't believe you, Himmy!"

"Sorry," said Himalette weakly.

"Why can't you leave things alone? You're going to get us both killed!"

"I'm sorry! I'm sorry!"

Brigitta sat up. "You couldn't keep your hands off that stupid flying beast, could you?"

"Whisper light," said Minq as if this cleared up the matter.

"Now all our supplies are gone—including the pages from Auntie Ferna's book!" Brigitta stared hard at Himalette. "And all our food."

"I didn't know!" Himalette sobbed.

"I knew you would get us into trouble." Brigitta stood up and brushed herself off. "I should have left you back home in a groven stench-bog!"

Himalette collapsed to the ground in tears. Minq wrapped his ears around her and patted her gently.

"Stop it, you big baby!" Brigitta turned away.

"No cry, little faerie." Minq lifted Himalette off the

ground and addressed Brigitta. "Follow Minq, please. We get new supply and food."

"From Gola?" Brigitta turned back around.

"She'll help?" Himalette lifted her head and wiped her nose with her sleeve.

"Gola see." Minq gestured with an ear toward a rough path into the forest. It was the first real path Brigitta had seen since they had left the Giant Caterpillar realm.

Without food or supplies, they had little choice but to follow Minq to Gola's. Brigitta signaled for Minq to lead the way and for Himalette to follow. Avoiding her big sister's glare, Himalette stumbled after him.

Brigitta glanced once more at Dead Mountain and sighed heavily, then turned to follow them down the path.

Chapter Eleven

As the forest grew darker, sleepy pairs of eyes appeared in the trees, watching them as they traveled. Himalette stopped to check out a wide split down the middle of a trunk. A growl from inside startled her and she ran to Brigitta, who shrugged her off, still fuming about the river incident.

Minq leapt over a fallen log. Himalette sullenly floated over it, then Brigitta flew over it, wincing as her injured wing knocked against a branch. She tumbled to the ground.

"Are you all right?" asked Himalette.

"I'm fine," Brigitta grunted. She picked herself up and motioned them along with a wave. They continued in silence. Brigitta cringed as her wing banged against another branch.

"Oh, no!" Himalette pointed into the trees. A fuzzy yellow light floated alongside them. It bumped into a tree branch and then danced over it.

"It all right, only whisper light." Minq motioned with his ear. "Come, come, very soon. Almost there."

Himalette caught Brigitta's eyes to let her know that she wasn't going to go running after the light. Brigitta took

Himalette's hand just in case and led her after Minq, who bounded ahead with a whooping bark.

Brigitta heard a soft hissing noise. She glanced around and through the trees. There was another hiss, slightly louder. Someone was whispering. She looked down at her sister.

"Stop it."

"Stop what?"

"That hissing. That whispering. Stop it."

"I wasn't whispering, honest." Himalette looked out into the forest. "I hear something, too."

Pssssss bssssss fsssss . . .

Two more fuzzy yellow lights appeared near her right ear. "Leave us alone," Brigitta growled and pulled Himalette away.

The rough path grew wider, more defined. It curved to the left, then the right, and then opened into a field of ochre colored flowers. It was brighter in the open field, but not much, as the sky was thick with muddy clouds. On the other side of the field, at the end of the path, stood an immense tree with an old knotted wood door and two small windows with faded curtains. Half-way up the trunk a tree-hole emitted a fine curl of smoke. Two more paths led off into the forest on either side of the tree.

Minq hopped up and down in front of the field. He motioned to them wildly and Brigitta had to smile. The tree looked homey and warm. She could smell something cooking, and she was more than famished.

As Minq stepped into the field, his leg glanced one of the flowers. It shivered a moment, then its petals dropped away, releasing the center of the flower into the air. The flower center caught the breeze and began to glow, first white, then yellow, like a little star. It drifted up and away.

Brigitta, still grasping Himalette's hand, made her way across the field. Minq trotted backwards shouting, "Come! Come!"

When Brigitta and Himalette were half-way across the field, a gust of wind sent flower petals whirling about. Dozens of fuzzy white star-lights floated from their stems. They turned from white to yellow as they drifted about. Himalette squealed with delight. Brigitta gripped Himalette's hand tighter and proceeded through the field.

"Ow!" complained Himalette.

Psssssst vssst . . . Brigitta could hear the whispers again. The yellow lights were everywhere, bombarding her. She shooed them away with her hand. The whispers grew more and more intense until the air was thick with them.

Psssst vrsst whhhhyyyuuu . . . stupid girl . . .

She could see them swirling across the length of the field. It sounded as if they were whispering directly into her ears. Her head began to thrum with sound. She wondered why Minq was still jumping up and down at the edge of the field. Could he not hear the whispers?

"Minq, stop them!" Brigitta finally pleaded.

"Come. Come. They say nothing." Minq gestured toward the tree. "Almost there."

Psssst vrsst whhhhyyyuuu stupid, stupid girl . . . all your friends are laughing at your empty wings . . .

"Brigitta, please!" Himalette yanked on her hand. "You're hurting me!"

84

Brigitta looked down at her hand; it was white from gripping Himalette's so hard. "Himmy, can't you hear them?"

"Yes, they're pretty. Like laughing."

She let go of Himalette, put both hands to her ears, and shut her eyes tight. "No, they're horrible and nasty!"

"They say nothing, please, come," Minq insisted.

Your momma turned to stone . . . your poppa turned to stone . . . Ondelle turned to stone . . . broken faeries everywhere . . .

"What do you mean? They're saying terrible things to me. You tricked me! You tricked us!" Brigitta's head echoed with the sound of the whispers, even with her hands over both her ears.

Minq grabbed Brigitta's arm and hauled her through the field. She stumbled along, arms flailing. He released her and she fell forward into the dirt. She opened her eyes to find she was staring at a twisted wooden cane. She followed the cane up.

A tall, thin being stooped over Brigitta. She was dressed in numerous folds of cloth and a tattered brown hooded cape. She removed her hood. Her skin was bark-like and her eye sockets were so sunken that Brigitta couldn't see any eyes. She tapped at the top of her cane with fingers of long, jagged twigs.

Himalette hid behind Brigitta who was still shaking the whispers out of her head.

The tree-woman stopped tapping and leaned into her cane. "What the ground creature means," she said in a gravelly voice, "is that the whispers indicate nothing."

"But—but," stammered Brigitta, "they knew things."

"Your mind will tell you what you want to hear."

Brigitta said nothing. She was certain those were not things she wanted to hear.

"Minq," the woman continued, "bring your . . . faeries inside." She hobbled over to the tree and slipped in through the door.

Minq's grimace-like smile appeared once again and he gestured toward Gola's home. Brigitta looked back at the field as the whisper lights drifted away, zigzagging against the darkening sky. She and Himalette made their way toward the tree while two pairs of wide eyes watched them from the forest.

A row of cauldrons filled with plants and herbs lined the path to Gola's door. As Brigitta and Himalette passed the cauldrons, several tiny violet flowers reached out and sniffed them.

"Chatterbuds. No hurt you. No say bad things," said Minq.

The plants greeted them in a tinny chorus, "Hello! Hello! Hello!" and eagerly waved their leaves.

Himalette reached out to touch one of them, then pulled her hand back and sulked. "I'm not allowed to make any friends," she said, nodding her head toward Brigitta.

"Sound advice in these forests," Gola's husky voice came from inside the tree.

Minq nudged the girls along with his ears, smiling to encourage them. Brigitta entered first with Himalette clinging to her from behind.

Gola's tree was surprisingly roomy. There was an unmade bed, a messy kitchen, and a laboratory piled with ancient books, vials of dark liquids, strange prickly plants, and jars of fermenting beasts. Dark splotches covered the inside walls of the trunk.

A small blue-gray pool of water, lined with stones, sat in the center of the floor. Gola tapped her way to the pool with her cane. Minq gestured for Brigitta and Himalette to sit down on the smooth stones and he sat down next to them, curling his long ears around himself like a shawl.

"What have you brought for me?" Gola addressed Minq as she faced the pool.

"Find sharmock root near caterpillar nest."

"Sharmock roots?" She turned toward him. "Very nice."

"But caterpillar catch me." Minq indicated Brigitta and Himalette. "Faeries save life."

"So no roots?" she inquired.

Minq shook his head sadly.

A pair of dark spots on the wall next to Himalette sprang open. It was a pair of Eyes. She shrieked and slipped off her rock. Brigitta pulled Himalette to her side.

The pair of Eyes flew from the wall on little bat wings and hovered in front of Minq. His face appeared in the blue-gray pool, wavering on the water as the Eyes fluttered about his face.

"Speak up, ground creature. I cannot hear you!" Gola commanded.

Minq looked into the hovering Eyes and smiled nervously. "No roots."

"Bah!" spat Gola and waved her hand at the pool.

Another pair of Eyes flew off the wall and joined the first pair. They swung around to examine the young faeries whose blue faces appeared in the pool. The Eyes studied Brigitta and Himalette's blue arms and legs and these images, too, materialized in the pool.

"What kind of faeries are you?" Gola asked.

"Please, your . . . tree-ness . . . we're Water Faeries," Brigitta's voice quivered. She held up her arm. "We're not usually, um, blue."

"What have I to do with Water Faeries?" Gola frowned and turned to the pool. The Eyes bobbed closer to the girls. "Have you run away from your forest?"

"Everyone in the White Forest is turned to stone," burst out Himalette, "and we have to go to Hrathgar's to find Blue Spell—"

"Himmy!" Brigitta hissed.

Gola spun around to face Brigitta and Himalette. "Blue Spell? Hrathgar has access to faerie Blue Spell?"

"You know about Blue Spell?" Brigitta asked.

The two pairs of Eyes flew up and landed on each of Gola's shoulders. "I have heard of it."

"Well," Brigitta paused, choosing her words carefully, "we don't know if she has it. We just know the White Forest has been cursed and, besides us, she's the only other faerie left."

"What makes you so certain Hrathgar will assist you?"

"She's kin! Faeries always help their kin. She's had such a long punishment. Maybe she's lonely and misses the

White Forest? Maybe ... maybe ... she feels bad about what she did?"

Gola grunted. "Of that I doubt. She is one who only serves herself."

"She's our only hope." Brigitta was on the verge of tears. "We have nowhere else to go. If we don't reverse the curse—if we don't turn everyone back soon—there won't be a White Forest."

Gola stood in silence, her two pairs of Eyes staring blankly ahead.

"It is a foolish idea," she finally said. She waved her hand and the Eyes returned to the wall. The images disappeared from the pool.

"Whether you help us or not," Brigitta said, "we're going to Dead Mountain."

Gola shuffled to her kitchen and felt her way to a large kettle that hung on a bar across a fire pit. A pair of Eyes dropped away from the kitchen wall and searched the jars of various herbs and roots until they found a glass container filled with shiny red stones.

Gola reached for the jar and removed one of the stones. She threw it into the fire pit and it burst into flames. The smoke danced and curled up the sides of the kettle and slipped through a crack in the tree-wall. Gola replaced the lid on the jar and the Eyes settled on top of it. They stared into the wisp of smoke as it escaped through the crack and Gola's barky brow wrinkled in thought.

"Hrathgar cannot be trusted," she said. The Eyes hopped over to the top of a jar of brown paste and peered into the kettle as Gola stirred its contents with a long spoon.

"However, she is highly skilled and may indeed possess a way of undoing this curse."

Brigitta stood up and moved to the kitchen. Himalette slid off her stone and curled up against Minq who wrapped one of his long ears around her shoulders.

A second pair of Eyes flew from the wall and across the counter until they came to a row of wooden cups. Gola grabbed one of the cups and sampled the brew from the kettle.

"You do not have the strength or knowledge to subdue Hrathgar. The only way would be to find her source of power and use it against her," she said.

"Can you help us, please?"

"I can see." Gola grabbed another cup and dipped it into the kettle. "But only on one condition." The second pair of Eyes landed on Gola's shoulder and blinked down at Brigitta. Gola handed the cup to her. "This land is too harsh for an old Drutan. I would prefer to live in your White Forest."

"But only the Elders can decide that," Brigitta said, taking the cup.

Gola gave a throaty chuckle. "Little faerie, if you succeed in tricking Hrathgar, than you are more than clever enough to convince your Elders to allow me passage into your forest."

Chapter Twelve

Brigitta and Himalette sat by the blue-gray pool watching Minq and Gola huddled in the entrance of her tree. Pointing a knobby finger into the forest, Gola dismissed a pair of Eyes from her shoulder and they flew off like a drunken bird. She held out her hand and Minq placed an ear in her palm. She whispered into his ear and he gave a nervous nod.

Everyone gathered around the pool. Several pairs of Eyes dropped from the walls and landed next to the murky water.

"Look here and see as I see." Gola pointed to the pool.

A wavering image appeared in the water. It was a bird's-eye view of The River That Runs Backwards. Avoiding its deadly pull, the Eyes flew high above the river which grew increasingly dark and tumultuous as it fought its way up the craggy mountain like a snaking storm. The river climbed up and up and then was sucked into the side of the mountain through an enormous cave.

"Where does the river come back out again?" asked Brigitta.

"Some say it goes to the Center of the World. Some say it emerges on the other side."

The pool reflected the mouth of the cave, then the inside, and then it grew dark.

"How strong are your wings?" Gola inquired, a pair of Eyes fluttering from the wall to examine Brigitta's blue-tinted wings.

Brigitta stretched them out, then winced. "One of them is torn."

Himalette fluttered her wings. "I have good wings!"

"I will take care of your injury and give you something for your strength," Gola said to Brigitta. She pointed at the image, indicating the mouth of the cave. "You will need to enter the cave here, otherwise, you will be attacked by Hrathgar's rock guards as you ascend the mountain or inhale some poison cloud. The river wind cleanses the air."

"I have no wings," Minq reminded her.

"The older faerie will carry you."

"We don't need Minq," Brigitta said.

"Minq will go."

A hazy greenish light appeared in the pool. As the Eyes moved deeper into the cave, the light grew brighter and soon they could see a much larger cavern with glowing crystals dotting the ceiling.

"When you reach the room of green zynthias," said Gola pointing to the green crystals, "you must quickly locate the entrance to the castle courtyard." Gola turned to Brigitta, and all the Eyes perched at the edge of the pool did the same. "Do not linger in this room or look directly into any of the crystals. They have an hypnotic effect and you may find yourself falling into a dream state from which you might never awake."

The pool reflected a dark cavity in the ceiling between two large crystals. Everyone watched as the Eyes entered the cavity, flew through a tunnel, and propelled themselves out of an opening in the ground. The water reflected a crumbling courtyard overgrown with thorny brush. Above the brush loomed the walls of Hrathgar's castle, greasy with slime and age.

The wavering image held for a moment, then suddenly vanished. Brigitta, Himalette, and Minq pulled back from the pool. The water returned to its original blue-gray state. All the Eyes around the pool shuddered.

"What happened?" Brigitta turned to Gola.

"Each time that is as far as I have seen." Gola motioned for the Eyes to lead her to her laboratory. "Perhaps you will fare better. The Eyes can see for me, but all alone they are defenseless."

"I've changed my mind. I want Minq to come with me. Himalette will stay here."

"But I want to come," said Himalette. "I want to help Momma and Poppa!"

"You wouldn't get past the zynthias, Himmy. You'd want to touch them or put them in your pockets."

"I won't. I promise I won't," she pleaded. "I'll show you. I'll be good from now on."

"You'll be good from now on and you'll stay here with Gola."

"Please don't leave me here!" Himalette looked up at Brigitta with large, watery eyes. "I want to go with you and Minq!"

"Your sister is right, little one." Gola motioned for Minq to get up. "It is far too dangerous."

Himalette sulked by the pool, dragging her hand through the water as Minq and Gola worked in the kitchen. A pair of Eyes landed on a jar and another landed on a stone measuring spoon. Minq gathered both items and presented them to Gola.

Brigitta wandered over to a shelf on the far wall piled with dusty books and broken pieces of red pottery. The books were a hodgepodge of shapes and sizes with strange symbols on their spines. She absent-mindedly scratched her blue neck as she followed the books to the end of the shelf. Next to the shelf, hanging on a tarnished silver hook in the wall, was a large stained and yellowed parchment with faded symbols.

It was a map of a continent, but its name was too worn to read. The continent was bordered on the west by a body of water labeled Sea of Tzajeek with a silvery spiny-backed serpent weaving through the letters.

Brigitta peered closer. On the southern part of the continent she could just make out the words Valley of Noe, the home of her ancestors and the Ancient Ones. She was looking at Foraglenn, the continent upon which they lived.

She looked to the northern end of Foraglenn and found the Dark Forest. A bare spot in the middle of the Dark Forest was labeled White Forest. In the middle of the bare spot was a miniscule hourglass no bigger than her pinkie fingernail.

To the east of the White Forest, a meandering line caught her attention. She guessed it to be The River That Runs Backwards. She followed it up to Dead Mountain where the line became dotted. The dotted line briefly went up, then turned sharply down and disappeared. It must be the river cavern, she thought, and then gasped.

Brigitta put her hand to her tunic pocket. Miraculously, the map she had stolen from her Auntie's book was still there. Without even looking at it, she knew the two maps had the same patterns and symbols. Gola's map must have been drawn by faeries.

Had Gola stolen it?

Brigitta poked at the map on the wall. "Where did you . . ." She stopped poking. There was nothing behind the map.

She lifted the map and it slipped from its hook on the wall revealing a hidden nook. Inside the nook sat four small red clay pots and an empty space where a fifth pot had previously been. Brigitta tipped the first pot and peeked inside. A round glassy object sat at the bottom. She reached in and took it out. It was like a piece of night sky.

She turned the dark stone around and around in her hand. Miniscule stars glimmered inside of it. As she stared into it, she felt her mind being pulled into the stars, drifting away . . .

Gola's gnarly hand swiped the stone away. Brigitta looked up to find several pairs of accusing Eyes hovering beside Gola's shadowy face.

"You will leave my possessions alone!" spat Gola returning the stone to the red pot and rehooking the map on the wall. She and the Eyes turned their attention back to Brigitta. Gola's empty wooden eye-sockets bore into her.

Brigitta opened her mouth to speak, but changed

her mind. She scooted away from the map and Gola shuffled back to her kitchen with all her pairs of Eyes except one, which stayed behind and sat themselves upon the dusty bookshelf.

Brigitta caught Minq giving her a strange look from the kitchen, but he recovered with one of his nervous toothy grins. She fluttered over to Gola's massive bed and dropped down onto it.

She closed her eyes and thought of her cottage in Tiragarrow, how light and warm it was compared to Gola's drafty tree. The wind outside made low musical sounds as it blew through the old, hollow branches. She imagined these to be the sounds of a new musical invention of her poppa's. A hollow tree that could sing. As she drifted off to sleep, she pictured his excited face as he proudly revealed his new creation.

🌑 🌑 🌑

Someone nudged the bed and Brigitta opened her eyes. Gola placed two large wrinkled black seed pods beside her. Brigitta sat upright and stared at the pods.

"What are those?" she asked.

"They are spell-seeds." Gola leaned on her cane as a pair of Eyes looked down from her shoulder. "For carrying potions and spells long distances." She patted a seed. "The contents are undetectable from the outside."

Brigitta took one of the seed pods from Gola and examined it. It was exactly like the one the White Forest sprite had been carrying—the one Brigitta had found later on the ground near the Hourglass and was now possibly traveling to the Center of the World inside of her pack.

"Just before you enter the cave, open the spell-seed and drink the root potion. It will give you enough strength to carry Minq through the cave and up to the courtyard," Gola said. "Do not drink it prematurely. Its effects are temporary. You will return to your own strength within four moon-beats, perhaps less."

"How do I open it?"

"Spin it exactly three times in the same direction as the sun and moons travel, then balance it on end and release three drops of water onto it. Tears will also work. Saliva will not, as it is impure."

"*Three turns . . . three tears . . . three turns . . . three tears . . . of wa-ter . . .*" Himalette sang as she appeared beneath them, craning her neck to get a better look.

"Be warned," said Gola, motioning for Minq, who brought Brigitta a woven pack, "when the effects of the mixture have completely subsided, there is a short period of paralysis, less than a moon-beat, but you will be helpless. Find somewhere safe to hide until the paralysis has worn off."

"What's pa-ral-sis?" asked Himalette, crawling up beside Brigitta. "Hey, Briggy, that's just like—"

"It means you can't move by yourself," Brigitta interrupted her sister with a glare. She placed the seed inside the pack. "Gola, do sprites use spell-seeds?"

"Sprites?" Gola looked surprised. She leaned forward. "I am the only one who knows how to construct a spell-seed. They are my specialty."

97

Gola thrust the second spell-seed at Brigitta. "What's this one for?"

"You will require it for your return." The Eyes flew back toward the kitchen and Gola followed. "You will leave with first light. Now we will tend to your wing."

Brigitta placed the second seed in the pack and jumped down off the bed. She caught Himalette's attention and put her finger to her lips. Himalette nodded in response.

As Gola straightened up her kitchen and prepared for bed, Minq took the girls outside to what he called his Dream Tree. "Night or day," he said, "good sleep in Dream Tree."

Ten steps from Gola's door, his Dream Tree was a smaller, squatter tree with a hollow L-shaped curve lined with soft beast fur. As they approached, its thick, crisp leaves rustled together in the wind. It sounded like the pitter-patter of rain. Himalette gasped in delight when she heard the rain-music of the tree and tugged on Brigitta's tunic. Brigitta was deep in thought.

"Sleep here." Minq patted the fur with his ear. "Be safe. Be warm."

Himalette climbed into the tree, curled up in the fur, and let out a tremendous sigh.

Brigitta set her new pack inside the tree. "What did Gola whisper in your ear earlier this evening by the door?"

"Not concern you." Minq looked her squarely in the eyes. "No matter."

Brigitta placed one foot into the tree and paused.

"And what's with those dark stones behind the map?"

"Shhhhh!" Minq took Brigitta by the shoulders and steered her into the tree. He leaned inside. "No touch Gola's moonstone. Only Drutan use. Very dangerous. Split your mind up." He tapped the side of his head with his ear.

"Well, I . . ." Brigitta paused. Himalette had stopped rolling in the fur and was listening to them.

"You sleep now," Minq said, and trotted back to Gola's tree.

The sisters curled up together in the warm fur.

"I don't trust her, not at all," said Brigitta. "Nor Minq."

"She scares me, Briggy," said Himalette. "I don't want to stay here."

Brigitta shifted so that the bandage on her wing was not directly under her shoulder. "We don't have a choice, do we?"

"I could go with you instead."

"No, Himmy, I might not be able to protect you up there."

"I can take care of myself," Himalette murmured.

Brigitta was quiet. She thought of her momma and poppa, of her auntie and her friends, and of Ondelle's beautiful cold stone face. She watched as the Great Blue Moon escaped from the clouds and the orange Lola Moon chased after it. She sank deeper into the layers of fur, lulled by the sounds of the gentle rain-music above.

Chapter Thirteen

Brigitta awoke to the yawning and chirping of the chatterbuds lining the path to Gola's door. It took a moment for her to realize where she was and that she was alone inside Minq's Dream Tree. She leapt out of the tree, raced to Gola's door, and burst inside.

"Himalette?"

Gola was startled out of bed. Winged Eyes dropped from the walls around her, hovering and blinking in a sleepy daze. Minq's head jerked up from the floor, his giant ears knocking a fluttering pair of Eyes across the room.

Gola snatched a shawl from the bedpost and threw it over her barky shoulders. "She is not with you?" she asked, all Eyes focused on Brigitta.

The three of them rushed outside and Gola sent a flock of Eyes into the forest. She stood there, concentrating, as Brigitta raced back to the blue-gray pool in the middle of the floor. There were too many images for her to sort out as the Eyes rushed past trees, down paths, out to the river. Branches and leaves and rocks sailed past at a dizzying speed.

"I can't see her! I can't see anything!" She rushed back to the door.

Minq stepped outside and spread out his ears. He rotated east, south, west, and north then shook his head. "No hear her either."

Brigitta zipped back to the Dream Tree to retrieve Gola's woven pack. She dumped out the contents. "She took one of the spell-seeds!" Brigitta cried. "She's gone to Hrathgar's on her own!"

"Then you must leave at once." Gola's flock of Eyes returned from the forest and everyone moved back inside. All of the Eyes flew to the wall except for one that landed on Gola's shoulder and blinked down at Brigitta. Gola removed a small pendant off a hook on the wall and placed it around Brigitta's neck. "Do not worry young faerie, you are much faster than she."

Brigitta glanced at the pendant. It was a small watery mirror. The pair of Eyes on Gola's shoulder hopped down to Brigitta's head and looked back up at Gola, whose face appeared in the pendant.

"And you will have my Eyes," Gola said.

Brigitta and Minq gathered their supplies and sped through the door. They were equipped with only a few essentials: food and water, healing bandages, branches treated with a flare spell, and the seed pod containing the strength potion. They did not want anything to slow them down.

Following a path leading away from the field of whisper lights, they tore through the forest as fast as they could. Brigitta's wings were much stronger than the day before, and she could fly swiftly when the path was wide enough. Minq leapt over logs and roots to keep up, using his ears to pull himself around trees. The Eyes followed them from above.

"It's all my fault." Brigitta ducked under a branch. "I was too mean."

"You only want keep safe," Minq panted back.

"She's just a little girl."

"We find her," Minq reassured Brigitta.

"Momma and Poppa will never forgive me if something happens to Himmy. Oh, lola!" Brigitta fought back her tears. What good would it do to save the White Forest if she had to go back and tell her momma and poppa she had lost Himalette? She thought about which horrible fates might befall her little sister. Sucked into the river-wind? Drowned in the cave? Eaten by Hrathgar's guards?

They broke through the forest onto an outcropping of rock and dropped into stunned silence as the massive shape of Dead Mountain loomed before them. The mountain was steep and jagged and barren. There weren't many places to hide from blood-thirsty beasts. Below them churned the unforgiving waters of The River That Runs Backwards. The river climbed the face of the mountain and disappeared. Farther up the mountain, she could just make out Hrathgar's castle camouflaged in the rocks and filthy air. The Eyes looked apprehensively at Brigitta and Minq.

Brigitta reached into her satchel and removed the spell-seed.

"Minq, if we use this one up, how will we get back?"

"Bigger problem first get *into* castle," Minq pointed out.

Brigitta nodded and placed the spell-seed on the

ground. She was about to spin it when Minq stopped her with an ear.

"No, too early."

"But I want to carry you up the mountain. You'll take too long without wings."

"Wait for cave," Minq insisted.

"Himalette could be in danger."

"If you paralyze in cave, we fall and drown. No help Himalette we dead."

Brigitta knew he was right. She put the spell-seed back into her pack and they began the steep ascent. There were no shadows to speak of, even though it was the middle of the day. It was too dark to cast shadows, but it wasn't clouds overhead that blocked out the daylight. The air itself was thick and dark. The darkness stuck to them as they made their way higher and higher. Brigitta's blue skin turned progressively gray, and her wings turned a sickly green. Minq looked as though he had been rolling in ashes and the Eyes had to keep blinking to shake the darkness off.

Brigitta sent the Eyes back and forth several times to check the distance to the cave. As they continued up the mountain, Minq slipped and slid on the rock slime and fell further and further behind. He's wasting time, Brigitta thought as she flew ahead. She could go much faster alone. Or even with Himalette, for that matter.

The top of the massive cave appeared over the rocks. The entrance to the cave was taller than the tallest tree Brigitta could imagine and as wide as the lyllium field outside of Tiragarrow. She could feel the pull of the river-wind as the water was sucked into the cave, inhaling the river like a giant mouth. She stopped short of getting caught in the suction and braced herself against a rock.

She looked out over what should have been a valley. She was high enough, she figured, to see the White Forest. But the darkness was too thick. The River That Runs Backwards shot out of it, toward the mountain, at a frightening speed.

She peered into the mirror necklace Gola had given her and panicked. The image was completely black. Then she realized this was simply because it was covered with a layer of soot. She looked up and spied the Eyes hovering high in the air in the entrance to the cave. Brigitta wiped off the mirror as the Eyes returned to her. They landed behind a rock and proceeded to clean themselves off with their little bat wings. When they were done preening, they sat and looked fixedly at Brigitta.

"Maybe she got scared and hid?" Brigitta regarded the Eyes. She knew Gola could only see her and not hear her, but she didn't know how much the Eyes themselves understood.

The Eyes blinked back at her.

Brigitta pointed out over the craggy mountain. "Go look for Himalette!"

The Eyes begrudgingly took off and fluttered in and out of the rocks while Brigitta watched in the mirror. Dark images flew past as the Eyes darted around, and then Minq's face appeared. She looked back up to see the Eyes fluttering toward her, followed by an exhausted Minq. He crawled up to her and collapsed on the ground.

"We can't stop now!" Brigitta cried. "What if she's

gone inside? We have to find her!"

Minq rolled over onto his back and groaned. "Why not see with Eyes?"

"Search the cave!" Brigitta pointed and the Eyes flew up high and into the cave. She watched the image of the menacing river churning and then saw cavern walls drenched with filthy water. It quickly grew dark, and there were a few harrowing moments of complete blackness before the strange glow of the green zynthias appeared.

"She'd want to touch the crystals. I know she would," Brigitta murmured.

Minq dragged himself over to Brigitta and peered into the necklace as the Eyes searched the cave walls and the angry water below.

"I don't see her. She's drowned!" Brigitta felt faint and dizzy.

"You not know she drown." Minq steadied her by the shoulders with his ears.

"Or fallen and hurt herself or been eaten by a—" Brigitta didn't even know what kind of beasts inhabited this place.

"Maybe she just turned to stone?" Minq offered.

Brigitta gasped and began to cry.

Minq wrapped an ear around her shoulder and she cast it off. She grabbed her pack and dumped out the remaining spell-seed. She placed it on the ground and spun it, counting as it turned, and stopping it after three revolutions. She stood it on end and collected the tears from her cheeks. She dropped them, one at a time, from her fingers onto the spell-seed.

"One for Momma . . . one for Poppa . . . and one for Himmy."

The spell-seed crackled. The top of it split open. Brigitta put it to her lips and drank the contents in one long gulp. She threw the wrinkled spell-seed into the river, where it was sucked away by the turbulent stream of water. With fierce determination, Brigitta pulled a flare branch from her pack, handed it to Minq, slung her pack over her front side, and leapt up.

"Get on."

Minq climbed aboard Brigitta's back and held on for dear life as she shot straight up, then into the cave. She flew near the top so Minq could strike the end of the branch on the ceiling of the cave. The ceiling was as sopping wet as the soggy walls. He struck it several times before the end of the branch lit up, cutting through the murky darkness. Brigitta's wings sliced through the air effortlessly.

"You strong," called Minq over the noise.

She scanned the water below. It was loud and mad, and no place for any beast, faerie or otherwise. She shuddered and concentrated on flying.

"No look down," Minq warned. "Make dizzy."

"Hold on, Himmy. We're coming."

They flew into a thick blackness so dark it absorbed everything save a disembodied flame on the end of the flare branch. If it weren't for the crashing of the water below, she wouldn't even have known which way was up.

She flew carefully until she could see the green glow of the zynthia cavern ahead. Looking for any sign of her sister, she focused her gaze on the walls of the cave. When they entered the zynthia cavern, the wind grew even more fierce as the river suddenly plummeted into an eternity of darkness. No doubt, Brigitta thought, on its way to the Center of the World.

She took a deep breath and sped toward the top of the cave. She hovered there, scanning the walls, as gusts of river-wind tossed them around.

"No look into crystals," Minq reminded Brigitta.

She couldn't stay still long enough to get a good look at anything. "I can't see her anywhere!" Brigitta shouted over the roar of the river.

"Maybe she find tunnel to castle! We look!" Minq shouted back. She flew to the far side of the cavern and combed the ceiling, careful never to look a green zynthia straight on. One of her wings faltered and she caught herself. "Minq!"

"What wrong?"

"You're starting to get heavy."

A fierce wind caught them and they dropped down toward the water.

"Must fly higher!"

"I can't! I can't!"

As they fell, Brigitta spotted a ledge in the rock wall. She maneuvered to it and landed to rest. Minq climbed down from her back.

She spit as the foul water from the walls splashed her face. "Where did the Eyes go?" She pulled out the mirror necklace and they both gazed into it.

Himalette's anguished face appeared in the mirror, crying out to them.

"Himmy!" Brigitta called and scanned the cavern. "Where are they? I can't hear her!"

"River too loud." Minq thrust out his ears and closed his eyes to concentrate. He twisted his ears in every direction. He opened his eyes again and pointed, "That way!"

Minq jumped up on Brigitta's back and she leapt into the air. Minq felt heavier than before, and her hands and feet were tingling. She mustered as much energy as she could and followed Minq's ear as it pointed the way to the far side of the cavern. Tucked behind some rocks, Brigitta could see Himalette waving to them frantically as the Eyes fluttered about her head. Brigitta landed behind the rocks and wrapped her arms around her sobbing sister.

"You're alive! Oh, Himmy!" She grasped Himalette tightly. She let go and drew back. "What were you thinking! How did you get here!"

"I—hid—in the forest—and followed you—I just —I wanted to—" Himalette managed to blurt out through her tears. "I can't feel my feet!" she cried.

Brigitta's own feet were now going numb. She shook them out.

"You lose strength, paralyze." Minq poked at Brigitta, "Must get out of cave."

"Minq, stay here," Brigitta commanded. "I'm going to get Himmy safe and then come back for you."

Himalette jumped on Brigitta's back. With a burst of strength, Brigitta leapt from the ledge and flew toward the ceiling.

"Close your eyes, Himmy."

Brigitta quickly scanned for the image she had seen

in Gola's pool, keeping her eyes slightly closed and out of focus so the zynthia hypnosis couldn't take hold. She felt for the cold spot in the ceiling Gola spoke of. She reached three zynthias the size of large mushrooms hanging in a triangle around a dark hole.

"I feel it! It's cold here!"

Brigitta flew through an opening just big enough for the two of them to slip inside. She felt her strength waning as she darted up the hole in the earth.

"Himmy, can you fly on your own now?" she asked.

Himalette slipped off her back and Brigitta took her hand. They flew up the crevasse until they were well out of the river-wind. Brigitta stopped and looked up. She could just barely make out the other side of the crevasse, a pin prick of sky in the distance.

"Himmy, listen to me," Brigitta said sternly, "you must get out of here."

"I can't," Himalette moaned. "I'm so tired."

Brigitta looked around. There were no hand or footholds in the crevasse, nowhere for Himalette to go when the paralysis took over.

"I have to go back for Minq before I lose all my strength," said Brigitta. The tingling sensation had crawled up to her knees and elbows. "Do you remember the image of the castle in Gola's pool?"

"Yes, I remember."

"Good girl. I want you to fly as hard and fast as you can out of this tunnel and in through one of those castle windows."

"I'm too scared!"

Brigitta knew she didn't have the energy to take Himalette to the castle and go back for Minq. And she couldn't risk going into the zynthia cavern without a strength potion. She shook her hands to relieve the tingling.

"Let's play a game. You like games, right?"

"Yes . . ." Himalette eyed Brigitta suspiciously.

"Pretend you're the fastest faerie in the White Forest. Fly into the castle as quick as you can, and then hide. I'll find you with Gola's Eyes! Okay? What are you going to do?"

"Go fast then hide."

"You can do this," said Brigitta. "Sing yourself a flying fast song. And find a really good hiding spot. Remember, you won't be able to move for a bit. But that's just part of the game."

"I'll sing about shadowflies. They're fast."

"Minq and I will be there soon. I promise. Go, now, quick!"

Himalette headed up the crevasse and Brigitta dove back into the cave for Minq. "If you're really there, somewhere," Brigitta said out loud to the Ethereals, "please protect my little sister. That's all I ask."

The tingling sensation had reached her hips and shoulders by the time she returned to the ledge. Minq jumped on her back and the exhausted Eyes gripped her right shoulder as she made one last journey to the ceiling. Minq pointed the flaring branch toward the crevasse. As she was about to enter, she felt Minq slump over on her back.

"Hmm . . . pretty," Minq sighed in her ear.

"What? Minq, you're slipping!"

"Pretty . . . pretty green." Minq began to laugh as

Brigitta struggled to keep him balanced. The Eyes leapt from Brigitta's shoulder and batted Minq's face with their wings. He laughed harder and dropped the flaring branch. It tumbled to the water below and vanished. Brigitta felt Minq's body slip from her back.

"No!"

"Whee!" he cried as he plummeted toward the water.

Brigitta dove after him with lightning speed and grabbed him by the ears. She flew back up toward the crevasse, the Eyes leading the way. She fought to keep her energy and focus as they disappeared inside.

Chapter Fourteen

With the delirious Minq weighing her down, Brigitta struggled after Gola's Eyes, hoping the strength potion would last long enough to get them up the narrow opening. Lit with a hazy green light from the zynthias below, it was less a tunnel than a large crack in the earth that had grown wide from the seasons of river rumblings below.

Before she knew it, they had burst through into the open air and were hovering in the middle of a decaying courtyard. The lawn and garden had long turned to dust and the only remnants of more fertile days were a few dry, thorny bushes along two sides of the walled courtyard. The third side looked out over the wall, thick with slime, onto the darkness below. The courtyard stood at the base of an imposing stone castle coated in layers of sludge.

Brigitta dropped to the ground in relief and Minq tumbled away from her. The Eyes fluttered around Brigitta's head and she waved her hand to let Gola know they had made it safely out of the cave. As she started to get up, the Eyes were yanked from the air and Brigitta watched in horror as they vanished into a gigantic frog's open mouth.

She jumped to her feet and stumbled. She could no

longer feel her left foot. The bulbous frog cocked its head toward her. It took a leap in her direction and she backed up, tripping over Minq.

"So that what happen Gola's Eyes," mused Minq dreamily, still under the spell of the green zynthias. He laughed and pointed at the approaching frog. "She feeding frogs."

"Minq! Come on!" Brigitta grabbed one of Minq's ears and pulled.

The frog leapt closer and opened its mouth. Its tongue shot out and wrapped itself around Minq's leg. The frog yanked Minq and Brigitta forward.

"Oh, no you don't, you oversized tadpole!" Brigitta yanked back and beat her wings with all her might. Minq continued to laugh as she and the frog fought their deadly a tug-of-war.

"Tongue prickly. Tickles!" He squirmed around on the ground.

Three more frogs appeared from the dark corners of the courtyard and hopped toward them. Brigitta pulled as hard as she could, but her strength was draining. Minq started to slip from her grasp. "Snap out of it, Minq!"

"I frog food!" Minq howled with laughter.

Brigitta gripped his ear desperately as they were dragged closer and closer to the giant frog's mouth. Minq's other ear swatted Brigitta in the face as he squirmed.

"Cut it out!"

"Wheeee!"

Brigitta grabbed a hold of his free ear and pulled both ears toward her face. "Miiiiiiiiinq!!!" She screamed as loud as she could into them.

He snapped out of his daze and shook his head. He looked up into the googly-eyed frog face. "Ahhhhhhh!" he shrieked and dug his paws into the earth.

Together they pulled against the frog's grasp, gaining a little ground. Another frog tongue shot out toward them, the first frog let go, and they toppled backwards. They leapt up again and Minq jumped onto Brigitta's back. She flew unsteadily toward the castle, dodging oncoming frog tongues.

Brigitta spotted a small window in the castle wall, high off the ground. She flew through the window and they spilled onto the cold hard floor. Minq sprang up on his hind legs, positioning himself for an attack. Brigitta struggled to get up, but her body was frozen. She lay on the floor unable to move.

Minq tried to lift her from under the arms. "You heavy like stone."

"Don't say stone," she winced.

"You heavy like . . . big rock."

"How long will I be paralyzed?" Brigitta could barely turn her head. The rest of her body felt like clay. She gazed across the ancient floor. She could see to the end of the dark, empty hallway and nothing else.

"Not know. At least frog too big come in window."

Voices echoed from somewhere inside the castle. They heard the shuffling of footsteps as a shadow appeared at the end of the hall. Minq gasped and frantically pulled at Brigitta from behind. His paws skidded and slipped on the floor. He ran around and grabbed her hands. He heaved and managed to pull her into a sitting position, but she couldn't move her legs. They weighed her down like two sacks of uul tree sap.

The shadow grew larger on the wall. Minq moved behind Brigitta and cowered under her wings, whimpering. He held onto her and covered his eyes with his ears. "No watch. Tell Hrathgar kill us quick."

Himalette's face appeared from around the corner and she squealed, "Briggy!"

"Himalette!" Brigitta was overcome with joy. "Oh, lola, I knew you could do it!"

Himalette flew into Brigitta, knocking her back over on top of Minq. She hugged Brigitta as Minq crawled out from under her. When Himalette pulled away, Brigitta examined her for injuries, noting a dozen cuts and bruises on her arms and legs. She motioned weakly for Himalette to lean down and she kissed her little sister on the cheek.

"You're not mad at me, Briggy?"

"I should be!" Brigitta scolded, and then quickly lowered her voice to a harsh whisper. "What were you thinking following us up here? You could have been killed."

"You were going to leave me all alone with Gola," Himalette said meekly.

"We'll talk about this later." Brigitta glanced down the hall. "Right now, you have to help Minq get me up."

"It's all right. The same thing happened to me," Himalette said proudly, and then burst into tears. "Oh, Briggy, I was so scared of the river. I remembered to make myself strong and I didn't look at the green lights, but I got tired and my feet paralyzed . . . and then you saved me . . . "

Himalette sniffed and wiped her eyes on her sleeves. "I went fast, like you said, and I landed in here and I was so cold and scared . . . and then Hrathgar—"

"Hrathgar?!?" gasped Brigitta and Minq.

Himalette grinned as a figure appeared at the end of the hallway and shuffled toward them. Minq wrapped one ear around Brigitta and the other around Himalette and growled. Brigitta stretched her head up from behind his ear and saw a kind-faced old faerie woman with shriveled wings. Whatever destiny markings she had been given as a youth had faded away. She wore a long red tunic woven with flowers. Her wild gray hair was piled on top of her head and her green eyes twinkled out from the crevices in her face. She bent over and examined Brigitta and Minq.

"This must be Brigitta. My goodness, you're as blue as your sister." Hrathgar reached out to touch Brigitta's face. Minq leapt forward and bared his teeth. Hrathgar took her hand away. "Oh, such a charming beast. And so protective."

"It's all right, Minq," said Himalette.

"Yes, yes," said Hrathgar. "You have nothing to worry about now. The frogs can't hurt you in here. Let me help you." She reached down to lift Brigitta from the floor. "Oh, you poor lolas."

"You're Hrathgar?" Brigitta studied the elderly faerie's face for signs of evilness.

Hrathgar smiled and assisted Brigitta to her feet. Minq moved to Brigitta's other side and assisted with his ears, watching Hrathgar's every move. Brigitta steadied herself with one hand on his head and one arm around Hrathgar. Himalette flew and danced around them as they shuffled down the corridor.

"Not only that, she says she'll help us!" cheered Himalette.

"Really?" Brigitta was astounded. "You can help us?"

"Well, I don't know," Hrathgar replied humbly. "I'll do what I can."

"She's going to help us save the White Forest!" cried Himalette. "We're going home!"

Hrathgar's kitchen was filled with herbs and roots and vegetables. It reminded Brigitta of her momma's kitchen and she was immediately comforted by the familiar smells. Once Hrathgar had Brigitta settled at the large wooden table, she went about making something to eat.

Brigitta's arms and wings were working again, but her legs were still numb. She and Himalette rubbed them briskly to get the feeling back. Brigitta tickled Himalette and they laughed together. It felt like a million moons since Brigitta had laughed.

They patted Minq on the head and played with his ears as he sat there like a guard, silently watching Hrathgar puttering about the kitchen. He ignored their teasing, even when Himalette called him "boggy breath" and "gundle toes," which sent the girls into new fits of giggles.

Brigitta felt warm and dreamy as Hrathgar returned to the table and dished out four healthy portions of root stew and four cups of tingermint tea. Brigitta and Himalette devoured their food. Minq sniffed at his dish and pushed it aside.

Hrathgar sat down with her guests. "It's so nice to have visitors who enjoy traditional faerie cooking."

"Do you get many visitors?" asked Brigitta, blowing on her hot tea.

"I don't think so. I—no." Hrathgar stopped eating and put down her spoon. Her eyes welled up with tears.

Brigitta stared at Hrathgar and the warm, dreamy feeling started to drain from her body.

Himalette kept slurping away at her stew. "I told her all about how we turned blue and about the broken faeries and the stone grovens and the Hourglass," Himalette said with her mouth full. "And how we need special faerie magic to turn everyone back."

"The only magic I know involves food and gardening," Hrathgar said, smiling weakly at Himalette and stroking her hair. "I have a wonderful potted crotia. And an entire row of gundlebeans."

"Your stew's delicious," commented Himalette, licking her bowl clean. "Almost as good as our momma's."

"I don't understand," Brigitta said finally.

Hrathgar turned toward Brigitta. Her eyes bore seasons of sadness.

"Why you not monster?" demanded Minq, startling the others.

"A monster? Oh, dear," said Hrathgar. "As far as I know I've always been a faerie." She looked over her shoulder and flapped her withered wings. "But as you can see, my wings are useless."

Brigitta examined them. It was true. They looked like old dried up leaves. Auntie Ferna had said Hrathgar had been marked for Elderhood and that was her path before she was banished. But where were her markings? Brigitta had never heard of any faerie straying from her Life Task. But there Hrathgar was, far away from the Council of Elders.

"Why did you have to leave the White Forest?" asked Himalette.

"Honestly, I don't remember much at all," Hrathgar sighed. "I know I did a very bad thing and was sent to live here. I know I've been here, alone in this castle, for a long, long time. But ask me the details of how I have spent my time? I do not know."

Brigitta thought about the faerie tales of Hrathgar's attempt to steal the power from the Hourglass. It was a very long time ago. Brigitta couldn't imagine this kindly faerie committing such a horrible act. Had they banished the wrong faerie? Brigitta knew Ondelle had been an Elder at the time. Surely the wise and just Ondelle would never have banished anyone unless it had been absolutely necessary.

"How we know you tell truth?" Minq pointed an accusing ear at Hrathgar.

"How do I know you're telling the truth?" Hrathgar pointed her spoon back at him.

"What do you remember?" asked Brigitta.

"My garden and kitchen." She gestured and smiled proudly at her roots and vegetables. "I know how to tend plants and herbs. That seems important."

"If you help us, maybe the Elders will forgive you and let you live in the White Forest again," suggested Himalette.

"I would like that very much." Hrathgar took Himalette's hand and gave it a squeeze.

They finished up their meal. Minq succumbed and took a few laps of stew. Brigitta gave him a smirk.

"Test make sure not poison." Minq lapped at the cup of tea a few times as well.

They withdrew to the castle's spell-chamber. It was crammed with potions and plants and dead beasts and dried powders and jars of strange liquids. Everyone, even Hrathgar, stood in the center of the room, not touching anything. Hrathgar moved to a podium on the far side of the room. She removed a massive, ancient book and brought it to the others. Everyone except Minq sat on the floor and gathered around the book. Minq wandered around, poking his nose into drawers and behind cabinets, keeping one ear cocked backwards and listening.

"I found this here this morning," said Hrathgar. "It looks useful. And several potions were brewing. I don't remember what they're for, though."

"You can make magic potions?" asked Himalette.

"I don't know." Hrathgar shook her head sadly.

"So you don't know anything about faerie Blue Spell?" Brigitta opened the book to the first page. The title was handwritten in a language she didn't recognize. The page was splattered with green and purple stains.

"Faerie Blue Spell?" Hrathgar gasped.

"Isn't that why we look this way? Isn't that how the sprite protected us from the curse?"

"You were most definitely protected by strong magic." Hrathgar studied Brigitta's blue skin. "But, I've never seen anything like this before. At least, not that I remember."

Brigitta's heart sank. "If we can't use Blue Spell, we'll have to find something in this book to reverse the stone curse. If we can get the Elders back to normal, they can reset the Hourglass."

Brigitta flipped through the pages of the book. The writing wasn't at all familiar. There were squiggly lines and small symbols similar to the ones on the spines of Gola's books. "I can't read this, any of it." Brigitta turned to the end of the book. "What is it? What does it say?"

"I have no idea," said Hrathgar as she pondered the book.

"You lie!" Minq was at Brigitta's side. "Someone wrote book. Someone make potions. You say you only one here!"

"I wish I were lying, Minq." Hrathgar pointed to one of the pages. "I wish I did know what this said. How do you think it feels to wake up in a room and not recognize the things around you?"

Minq tapped the book. "This Dark Forest language." Minq looked Hrathgar squarely in the eyes and scowled at her. "Someone teach you."

"I don't know!" She cried and then dropped her head into her hands. "I don't remember."

"Perhaps forgetting is part of your punishment?" Brigitta suggested. "So you wouldn't be able to . . . you know . . . do your very bad thing again?"

"Yes," Hrathgar said solemnly. "That's it. I'm sure you're right. I'm being punished."

"If we can't read this, we'll never be able to save the White Forest." Brigitta slammed the book shut in despair.

"The Hourglass runs out at night's end!" Brigitta leapt up and flew to the window. "As soon as the moons have left the sky," she murmured. She could just make out a faint glow behind the dingy air and clouds. How much time did they have? Less than twenty moon-beats; she was sure of it.

"Momma and Poppa," whimpered Himalette.

"I'm so sorry." Hrathgar put her arm around Himalette, who started to cry. "Isn't there anyone else we can go to for assistance?"

"There aren't any other faeries left. We're the only—" Brigitta slapped her forehead. "Wait! Minq, you said this was Dark Forest language. Do you think Gola could read this spell book?"

Minq twitched at the mention of Gola's name. "It possible." He eyed Hrathgar as her brow wrinkled in thought.

"Then I'll take it to her."

"No strength potion," he pointed out. "River wind too strong in cave."

"I'll fly outside, down the mountain."

"Too dangerous," said Hrathgar. "The frogs are not the only beasts guarding this castle."

"We have to do something!" exclaimed Brigitta. "We're running out of time."

The room went silent. Minq paced back and forth while Hrathgar rocked Himalette in her arms and Brigitta tapped her wings together, like her poppa.

"If only Gola could see," said Brigitta.

"Briggy, the Eyes can see!" Himalette suddenly perked up. "Where did they go?"

Brigitta pulled out her mirror necklace and peered into it. It was completely black. "Frog food," she muttered.

Minq's ears darted into the air. "You have sharp knife?" he asked Hrathgar.

"Yes, in the kitchen."

"Give me. Have idea."

Chapter Fifteen

Brigitta, Himalette, Minq, and Hrathgar stood at the edge of the courtyard. The sky above was bleak. The last light on the horizon was smothered by the dreary haze. The shrubs lining the courtyard walls stood like dark, disfigured skeletons. As her eyes adjusted to the dimness, Brigitta caught sight of several large bulbous frogs sitting in the weeds. The frogs cocked their heads toward them. Hrathgar pulled Himalette to her side. Minq held out the large sharp knife he had retrieved from Hrathgar's kitchen.

"How can we tell which frog it was?" Brigitta scanned the courtyard. "They all look the same to me."

"Will know." Minq's ears shot out toward one frog, then another, as they hopped toward them. "He sound mean."

"They all sound the same, too," muttered Brigitta.

"Shhhh." Minq's ears stopped moving. "There, see," he said, "next to tunnel in ground."

Mean Frog hopped closer into a square patch of faint light drifting down from the castle. His slimy face was briefly illuminated before he hopped out of the light again. Brigitta had no idea how to tell the difference between the sounds of frog hops, but she had to admit that its face looked familiar, and mean, with its large blood-shot eyes and snotty nostrils.

"Ready?" she whispered to Minq.

Minq nodded. Brigitta flew through the air zigzagging toward the frog. It stopped hopping and its eyes rolled around as she zipped past it. It opened its mouth and zapped its tongue at her, missing by a wing's length.

"Missed me, bog-breath. Ha-ha!" Brigitta circled back again.

Two more frogs joined Mean Frog. Their tongues flew out at her and she dodged them both, heading straight for the first frog. As she turned, its tongue darted past her ear.

The smallest of the three frogs suddenly stopped and turned back toward the castle.

"Hey! Up here!" Brigitta called. "Up here you slimy, green—"

"Haaaaaaaayaaaaaaaaaa!" Minq leapt through the air. He landed on Mean Frog's bumpy back and wrapped his ears around its belly to secure himself. He lifted the knife over his head . . . ZAP! a frog tongue wrapped around his arm. The tongue belonged to an extremely fat frog with spindly front legs that had joined the other three.

Before Minq could brace himself, he was yanked off of Mean Frog's back and dragged across the courtyard toward Fat Frog's mouth.

Himalette and Hrathgar cried out from the edge of the courtyard. Brigitta looked up as Himalette tried to fly out of Hrathgar's grasp.

"Stay there, Himmy!" yelled Brigitta as she dodged another tongue.

"Heeeeeelp!" shrieked Minq as he dug his back paws and ears into the dirt.

Himalette wriggled out of Hrathgar's grasp and flew into the courtyard.

"Himalette, no!" Hrathgar pleaded. She flapped her useless wings and ran after Himalette. Three menacing frogs leapt toward her. She retreated back to the castle, wringing her hands together as she watched the frightening scene from behind a pillar.

Himalette dropped down to the ground and picked up a rock. She launched herself over Fat Frog and dropped the rock solidly on its head. It retracted its hold on Minq's arm and Minq went tumbling backward, feet over ears, the knife flying out of his hand. A purple frog and a brown frog paused at the knife and looked down at it curiously.

"Himmy, get out of here!" Brigitta turned and scolded Himalette.

"I'm helping!" Himalette dove down to pick up more rocks. She chucked them at Purple Frog and Brown Frog, stunning them long enough for Brigitta to fly down and pick up the knife.

"Over here, Mean Frog!" Brigitta somersaulted through the air.

Minq pulled himself up and steadied his dizzy head. He spotted Mean Frog and glanced around desperately. Brigitta whistled from above and dropped the knife. He caught it with an ear, took a deep breath, and catapulted himself onto Mean Frog's back. He drove the knife into its back with a sickening crunch. A dark greasy fluid gushed forth. He twisted the knife and the frog sunk to the ground, fouling the air with a nasty belch.

Brigitta joined Himalette, dodging tongues as they picked up rocks. They smashed them over frog heads as they hopped toward Minq. He leapt off of Mean Frog and with great effort, heaved it over onto its back. He jumped onto its stomach and bounced up and down on all fours.

"Hurry, Minq, we can't hold them off!" Brigitta called as two more frogs hopped over the castle wall and cocked their heads.

"Ohhhh!" a voice cried from behind them.

Brigitta glanced toward the castle. The three frogs were still there, but Hrathgar was gone. Brigitta flew across the courtyard. "Hrathgar?" she called.

"Frog stink bad," Minq grumbled.

Hrathgar wasn't behind the pillars. The three frogs turned and leapt toward Himalette. Brigitta dashed toward her sister, grabbing her hand and pulling her higher into the air.

Minq bounced up and down on Mean Frog's stomach. With a whoosh of air the Eyes popped out of the frog's mouth. Brigitta swooped down and caught them, dripping green slime all over herself.

"I've got them!" she cried as a frog tongue wrapped around her leg.

Minq dashed forward, sliced the frog tongue away with the knife, and grabbed a hold of Brigitta's other leg. Himalette joined them and they soared out of the courtyard, Minq clinging to Brigitta's calf. He threw the knife down at

127

the frogs and hit one in the thigh. They flew through a high window as frog tongues blatted against the castle wall.

They fell to the floor with a great thud, with Brigitta on the bottom of the pile and Himalette on top.

"I hate frogs," Himalette said to the floor.

"Think hurt something," said Minq, sandwiched between the girls.

"Yeah, me," Brigitta heaved. "Get off!"

Himalette rolled over, then Minq. Brigitta sat up and handed him the Eyes. He shook them gently. They were limp and lifeless and covered in frog juice. Brigitta looked at them skeptically as she rubbed frog slime from her leg.

"Will work," Minq said, tucking the Eyes into his left ear and scrolling it down to protect them. "Need soak in water with lyllium nectar. Need lyllium blossom."

Brigitta got up and dusted herself off. "Lyllium blossom? Where are we going to find lyllium blossom on this rock heap, let alone figure out how to get nectar from it?"

"You forget, Hrathgar master gardener."

"Hrathgar!" Brigitta exclaimed and rushed to the window. All the frogs below were slowly hopping toward the dead body of Mean Frog.

Hrathgar was nowhere in sight.

Chapter Sixteen

Minq and the faerie sisters raced back to Hrathgar's spell-chamber and in through the door. Brigitta felt a rush of relief. Hrathgar was bent over the podium, her back to them as she examined the spell book.

"Hrathgar!" exclaimed Brigitta collapsing to the ground and catching her breath. "We got the Eyes! All we need is—"

Hrathgar turned around and Brigitta's skin went ice cold. Hrathgar's face was yellow and leathery and her eyes were blood-red. She drew herself up to her full height and grinned at their bewildered faces, teeth rotting inside her shriveled mouth. "Hello, my dear faerie kin."

"Hrathgar, what happened to you?" Himalette's voice shook.

Hrathgar moved to the nearest window and peered out the dingy curtain. "So close to night's end," she sighed. "Such sweet news to a long suffering outcast." Hrathgar flung the curtain back to reveal the two moons, wild and bright, through an opening in the sinister clouds. "When the moons leave the sky the White Forest will lose its protective field." She took a step toward them and pointed a knotted finger. "And I will take over as the new High Priestess."

"What I say?" growled Minq. "She lying whole time."

"But what about—" Brigitta started to say.

"Silence!" Hrathgar commanded as she dropped the curtain back down. She glared at all of them. "Three hundred seasons of this disgraceful existence have allowed me to develop my . . . talents."

"You're the one who turned everyone to stone!" Brigitta gasped. "But how?"

Hrathgar cackled and took two steps toward them. They all took two steps back. "Through a little trick of green zynthia hypnosis on an unfortunate sprite I caught before my frogs got the best of her." She squinted her eyes at the two faerie girls. "Judging by the color of your skin, it seems that someone managed a little trick of their own." Hrathgar reached over to her collection of potions. She selected a beaker of deep crimson liquid and turned back to them, raising her crooked eyebrows. "Tell me, how did you get your blue?"

As Hrathgar leaned forward Brigitta noticed around her neck, hanging on a silver chain, a black stone with glistening stars. Minq stiffened beside her as he spied the amulet, too. Brigitta stared into it, her mind drifting.

"Tell me!" Hrathgar threw the beaker to the ground, startling Brigitta. As it shattered, red liquid splattered across the floor. Each drop began to hiss and fizzle as it burned into the stone.

"Brigitta!" Minq tossed the Eyes to her and rushed at Hrathgar. "Fly! Escape!" he shouted.

Brigitta caught the Eyes and grabbed Himalette by

the hand. Minq leapt toward Hrathgar and she snatched him mid-air, wrapping her hand around his neck. His eyes bulged as she squeezed.

"Fool," she grumbled, and then laughed. She called after Brigitta and Himalette as they flew from the room in a flurry of wingbeats. "There is no escape for you!"

Brigitta and Himalette darted down one dark corridor and through another. They turned a third corner, and then dropped to the floor and listened. Nothing.

Brigitta held up the lifeless Eyes. She ripped the remaining sleeve from her tunic and carefully wrapped the Eyes in it before tucking them in her pocket.

"Briggy, we can't leave him!" Himalette tugged at her sister.

"I know."

"We have to help him!"

"I know!" Brigitta snapped. "Let me think."

Himalette pulled her legs to her chest and wrapped her arms tightly around them, singing nervously to herself while Brigitta peeked around the next corner. Not two hops away, sitting at the bottom of a staircase, was a giant frog. Brigitta gasped and pulled back. She pressed Himalette up against the wall and signaled for her to be still.

Nothing happened.

Brigitta waited a few moments, puzzled. She slowly peeked around the corner again. The frog hadn't moved. Brigitta waved her hand and the frog just sat there. She squinted up the dark hallway, breathing a sigh of relief as she realized the frog had been turned to stone. As her eyes adjusted to the darkness, Brigitta saw that stone beasts of every kind were sitting on nearly every step. There were rodent-like creatures, bird-like creatures, little horned creatures, more frogs, and a smattering of beasts that were half stone, half decaying skeleton.

"All stone . . ." she murmured.

Himalette peered around the corner and gave a little cry. "Why, Briggy?"

"Practice." Brigitta grabbed Himalette's hand and they wandered up the staircase, past the stone beasts standing at attention. Half-way up, they came to a window.

"Maybe I can fly around the back of the castle and in through her spell-chamber window?" Brigitta mused. It was a dangerous plan, she thought, but a surprise attack would be best. Perhaps Hrathgar would leave the room in search of them with Minq locked inside? She could fly in through the window and grab him.

"You'll have to come with me. I can't leave you here by yourself." Brigitta studied her little sister's tear-streaked face. "You must do exactly as I say, when I say it, without any questions."

Himalette agreed as she wiped her dirty nose with her sleeve.

They flew out the window into the cold night. They were much farther from the ground than they had anticipated, and the sheer drop startled them both. Large jagged rocks rose from the ground below.

They flew high along the castle close to the walls. When they turned to fly along the back side of the castle, butting up against the sheer mountainside, they were greeted by several colorful gardens built on immense stone terraces jutting out from the castle walls. The plants and flowers were the only things outside the castle that remained unsullied by sticky darkness. As they rounded the next corner, they slowed and dropped down past the first darkened window.

Brigitta stopped and pointed toward the second window, which cast a yellow glow out into the gloom. She motioned for Himalette to stay back and keep quiet. Himalette nodded and hovered in the air.

Brigitta's heart pounded in her chest as she inched her way toward the second window. Steadying herself with carefully placed wingbeats, she maneuvered below the window and grabbed hold of its crumbling rock frame.

"Ha!" came Hrathgar's voice from inside the castle, startling Brigitta. Her hand slipped and she fluttered her wings to catch her balance. She pulled herself close to the wall.

"You are in no position to bargain with me," Hrathgar continued.

"It not belong you first place," came Minq's hoarse voice. "No good do you. No need."

"Perhaps I have grown used to it," Hrathgar snorted.

"It valuable only Gola."

"How valuable?" Hrathgar's voice grew serious.

"Her life depend on it."

"Then I am sure it is worth the Blue Spell magic of your two young faeries."

The wind suddenly picked up and Brigitta was blown away from the window frame. She heard a muffled cry from Himalette and looked down to see her sister picked up by a strong gust and sent tumbling toward the rocks. Brigitta fought the wind and sped toward Himalette. She caught up with her and they were both thrust into the castle wall. They spun against the hard stone, the wind whipping and howling around them.

As Brigitta and Himalette struggled to steady themselves, one of the immense rocks stretched up and opened its eyes. It lifted its long, rocky tail and craned its head toward them for a closer look. Himalette opened her mouth to scream, but Brigitta stifled it with her hand. The rock creature snorted and a storm of pebbles rained down on them.

Brigitta yanked her sister by the arm and they flew along the side of the castle as close to the ground as they dared. They turned the corner and there stood another rock beast, stretching its neck and yawning loudly. Its sharp silver teeth glinted in the moonslight.

"Briggy!" screamed Himalette over the howl of the wind.

Brigitta dove down and maneuvered between the beast's legs with Himalette fluttering madly behind her. She spied a small opening in the wall at the base of the castle and zipped toward it. The rock guard bounded after them and with each heavy step the jarring sound of rock hitting rock echoed off the mountain. Brigitta and Himalette dove through the opening in the wall. The rock guard rushed at the entrance, banging its head against the castle and blowing hot angry dust from its nostrils.

Just inside the castle, huddled in a dark tunnel, Brigitta and Himalette caught their breaths. The beast smashed against the castle wall once more and then shuffled away with one final snort. After it was gone, the only sounds were the wind whipping through the tunnel and the water dripping from the slimy walls. They exhaled in relief.

"Wha—what—was that?" Himalette asked in a shaky voice.

Brigitta seized Himalette's hand and pulled her along the wet passageway.

"Where are we going?" whispered Himalette.

"I don't know," answered Brigitta through clenched teeth.

"What are we going to do?"

"I don't know!"

"I'm scared," Himalette whined as she struggled to keep up with Brigitta.

"Himmy!" Brigitta glared down at her sister.

Himalette started to cry. She gave a great heaving sob and yanked her hand from Brigitta's. Brigitta turned away and marched up the passageway. I'm a bog-brain, she thought to herself. Minq was a traitor! Gola had sent him to Hrathgar's to trade them for a stupid black rock!

Brigitta slowed her pace. It all made sense now, she thought. Why would Gola help them, after all? She had sent her Eyes many times to find her precious moonstone and they had failed. She must have been thrilled when Brigitta told her she wanted to go to Dead Mountain. Minq might belong to them, but he had belonged to Gola first.

Brigitta stopped and twitched her wings. How had Hrathgar gotten the moonstone in the first place? And what about the spell seed she had given the hypnotized sprite to get a curse into the White Forest? Gola had said she was the only one who could make spell-seeds. Had Gola given Hrathgar the spell-seed? What if they had planned to curse the White Forest together and Hrathgar had double-crossed her?

Himalette's sobs grew fainter behind her. Serves her right, Brigitta fumed. They wouldn't be in this mess if Himalette hadn't made her lose all their supplies in the river. And if Himalette had been paying attention, she wouldn't have gotten caught by the caterpillar. She couldn't leave anything alone! Brigitta started up the tunnel again. Her sister's cries grew more desperate. Brigitta kicked the cavern wall.

Pippet's disapproving face appeared in her mind. She thought of her momma and poppa turned to stone in the White Forest and that she might never see them again. They would want her to take care of her little sister. They would want her to comfort her. They would be ashamed of her for leaving her behind. Himalette was just a child and she couldn't help herself. It wasn't her fault their home had been cursed.

"I'm sorry, Momma. I'm sorry, Poppa." Brigitta rushed back to Himalette, who was lying on the floor of the cold, damp tunnel with her head in her arms.

"Come on. Get up." She tugged at her sister.

Himalette sniffed and allowed herself to be picked up. "Where—"

Brigitta placed her hands on Himalette's shoulders and looked into her eyes. "Just come on. I'll figure something out."

They moved down the passageway toward a pale

light and emerged in a large cold room. There were several metal cages in the middle of the floor, with spiky bars, and four prison cells lining the walls. Fur and bones of long-dead beasts rotted in two of the cages. The cells held the remains of half-stone beasts; one with a small stone head and a body with decaying limbs, another with a skull stuck on a stone neck with stone legs and one stone arm. The smell of rotting flesh hung like fog in the dungeon room. Brigitta turned away from the dead beasts. "Don't look, Himmy."

A few large rodents scurried about, with menacing front teeth, long black tails, and matted brown fur. Brigitta threw a rock at one of them and it looked at her dully before skulking off. The girls tip-toed across the dungeon floor. As they passed the last cell a figure moved in the dark. They jumped back as Hrathgar emerged from the shadows.

Chapter Seventeen

Hrathgar's eyes lit up when she saw them, her face kind and soft again. "My dear girls! I am so glad to see you!" She clasped her hands together.

"Hrathgar!" exclaimed Brigitta and Himalette.

One of the mangy prison rodents scuttled toward them. Himalette squealed as Brigitta picked up a rock and threw it at the beast.

"Ignore the bone-dwellers. They are only interested in what is already dead."

Himalette stepped closer to the cell. "Hrathgar, how did—"

Brigitta placed her hand on the top of Himalette's wing to stop her. "Stay back, Himmy, it's a trick."

"It is a trick indeed," Hrathgar nodded. "But you needn't fear me."

"Who are you?" Brigitta demanded, keeping her distance.

"I am Hrathgar Good."

"There are two Hrathgars?" Himalette asked.

"We are one, split in two. Pure good and pure evil. Between night and day and day and night, we exchange places."

138

"Briggy, we have to let her out." Himalette moved toward the cell bars.

"Stay back!" commanded Brigitta.

"Where is your friend?" Hrathgar peered around the room.

"He was captured by the mean Hrathgar!" exclaimed Himalette.

"Minq is no longer our friend," spat Brigitta.

"No!" Himalette turned and looked incredulously at Brigitta. "He's our friend. We have to help him."

"Himalette, listen to me." Brigitta pulled her from Hrathgar's cell. "When I was at the castle window I heard Minq and the other Hrathgar arguing about Gola's moonstone. He wants to trade us for it."

"No!" insisted Himalette. "He's ours! He wouldn't let anybody hurt us."

"That's enough! You didn't see it at Gola's. Her moonstone is really valuable. She couldn't find it with her Eyes, so she sent Minq up here with us to get it back."

Himalette shook her head.

Hrathgar Good slumped to the ground and groaned. "Oh no. Oh no, no. It is all my fault. Brigitta, listen, please . . . Gola would not trade you for her moonstone."

"So, you admit it. You know about Gola and her moonstones."

"Yes, yes," moaned Hrathgar Good. "I was the one who stole it from her. Among other things."

"Like her spell-seeds?" Brigitta accused Hrathgar.

Hrathgar nodded sadly.

139

"Why?" Himalette asked.

"Selfish reasons." Hrathgar Good's eyes filled with tears. "I was young and full of myself. I was going to show the Elders how clever I was. I ran away from the White Forest, but didn't make it far before I had to be rescued by Gola."

"Three hundred seasons ago?" asked Brigitta.

"Yes. Gola was so pleased to have saved a faerie. She nursed me back to health and I lived with her for quite some time. She taught me many things about plants and potions.

"But she held things back. She said I was not ready. So I stole several of her belongings, including one of her moonstones, and returned to the White Forest."

"Minq says the moonstones are dangerous," said Brigitta as she moved closer to Hrathgar Good's cell.

"Dangerous for anyone other than their rightful owner," said Hrathgar. "It split my mind up. My mind became two minds. Two voices, good and evil, fought in my head until my evil mind tried to put a spell on the Hourglass of Protection."

"What happened?" asked Himalette.

"The Hourglass defended itself! Since I was wearing the moonstone, I was divided into two Hrathgars. The Elders banished us both here to Dead Mountain."

"That's terrible!" cried Himalette. "They should've kept the good you!"

"They had no choice."

"Auntie Ferna never told us the whole story," Brigitta murmured to herself.

"Fernatta of Gyllenhale?" Hrathgar Good smiled. "How is my old friend?"

"She's turned to stone!"

Hrathgar Good slumped again. "Oh, I am so sorry."

"You said you didn't remember anything except your garden," Brigitta accused.

"That is the doing of Hrathgar Evil. She imprisoned me, but as we exchange places when the day transitions, she is imprisoned half of the time as well. She cast a spell so that by day I would not remember anything except how to cook and garden. She did not want me to try to harm her or myself. And as she and I are one, she spends her days in this cell, dreaming of sharmock roots and wondering why she is behind bars."

Hrathgar Good's eyes widened. "But when she roams the castle at night, and I am here, we remember everything. She seeks a way to destroy me that will not destroy her along with it."

"Oh no!" Himalette gasped.

Brigitta stood there contemplating Hrathgar's story.

"You can count on Gola, I swear upon the Hourglass." Hrathgar moved forward, an intense look upon her face. "Of course she wants her moonstone back. When I stole it, I stole her destiny. She is a solitary being, but not cruel-hearted. She most likely found it difficult to trust you."

"I don't know." Brigitta stepped closer and examined Hrathgar Good carefully.

Hrathgar gazed into Brigitta's eyes. "Be careful of the bars. They will burn you."

Brigitta reached out and lightly touched a bar. She drew back as the bar singed her finger and gave off a little puff of black smoke. She sucked on her finger and eyed

Hrathgar suspiciously.

"Don't you believe her?" Himalette asked.

"There's only one way to find out," decided Brigitta, pulling the wrapped up Eyes gently from her pocket. "Hrathgar, do you know where we can get lyllium blossoms?"

Chapter Eighteen

Brigitta made her way back through the passageway. When she reached the entrance, she poked her head out to see if the coast was clear of nasty beasts. She quickly reached outside and grabbed two rocks.

"Take two rocks and knock them together in a slow, steady beat," Hrathgar had told her. "It is a lullaby to the rock dragons."

Brigitta clicked her rocks together a few times to steady her rhythm. Rock dragons, she thought, so that's what they were. She hoped when all this was over she'd never have to see one again. Not even in a dream.

Brigitta sang a traditional faerie lullaby to help keep tempo.

> *Lola Moon you've come too soon*
> *My eyes are not yet tired*
> *Great Blue Moon I ask of you*
> *Please chase your sister away*

She flew slowly along the castle wall, knocking her rocks together and singing to herself. A sleepy rock dragon lifted its head, snorted, and then lay back down with a small avalanche of pebbles. Brigitta continued along until she reached the back side of the castle where one of the large terraces jutted out half-way up the side.

Brigitta landed and made her way to the garden path which lead right up to the mountain and overlooked the endless rock dragon fields on either side. The garden was an oasis in the gray, with dozens of rows of plants and flowers of all shapes and sizes illuminating the sooty air. In front of the garden was a work station of stone shelves stacked with pots and piled with soil. A few gardening tools hung from a wooden plank.

Brigitta fluttered over and poked around the shelves until she found a spell-seed tucked into a nook where Hrathgar Good said one would be. Something scurried across the garden. Brigitta froze for a moment. "It's just a little garden beastie," she told herself and placed the spell-seed into a sack hanging next to the tools. She wrapped it with some twine and pulled it tight.

She moved to the right side of the garden. "Three rows down, one, two, three." She turned and moved along the third row. "Four plots over . . . " Brigitta felt a rush of relief as she spotted the leafy lylliums with their delicate white blossoms.

If it weren't for the urgency of her task, Brigitta might have enjoyed pulling the blossoms off the lyllium plants, allowing them to soothe her into a daydream. She smelled the blossoms carefully to see which ones were ready. Hrathgar had said that as lylliums grew less fragrant on the outside they grew more potent on the inside, and that the best lylliums for potions had no scent whatsoever.

As Brigitta was about to collect an odorless blossom, the sleeping thorny plants in the next plot over woke up and shook their leaves. "HEEEELP! Thief! HEEEEEELP!" they shouted from their large-lipped purple bulbs.

"Shhhhh!" Brigitta scolded, "I'm not a thief. Hrathgar Good sent me."

"HEEEEEEEEEEEELP! Somebody HEEEEELP!" they screeched.

Brigitta grabbed one of the shrieking plants by the stem and pricked herself on a thorn. "Ow!"

"Hee-hee-hee!" they squealed in delight. "Serves you right, thief. Heeeeeeelp!"

"Stop it! Be quiet!"

"Heeeeeeeeeeeeeeelp!" they cried out as they bounced up and down.

"Hush! You'll wake the rock dragons!" Brigitta kneeled down in front of them. "What do you want? Tell me whatever it is. I'll do it."

"Heeeell—" they stopped and turned to her slyly. "Really?

"Yes, anything to shut you up," Brigitta hissed.

The bulbs huddled together and whispered among themselves.

"Please hurry!"

They stopped whispering and sang out in a chorus, "Gwenefire!" Then they began to whistle and hoot loudly and rustle their leaves. "Oooooowooooo!" they called like a pack of wild beasts.

"Gwenefire?" Brigitta searched her gardening lesson memory bank. "Oh, please stop that racket," she cried to the munshmins as they continued to howl.

Brigitta got up and hunted through the rows of plants and flowers. "Gwenefire, gwenefire," she mumbled over and over, nearly in tears by the time she reached the eighth row.

Then she heard a soft giggling. That was it! *Giggling Gwenefires* her mother sometimes called them when she and Himalette had an unstoppable fit of laughter. She ran through the next row and there they were, with long lavender flowers and lashes and spots of pink on what could have been cheeks, giggling like a group of faerie girls.

Quickly and carefully, Brigitta dug up and transferred the gwenefires. She patted the ground around them as the purple bulbs purred. "Sweet gwenefire!" they sighed.

The gwenefires giggled and batted their lashes. The plants snuggled up against each other. "Ooh!" the gwenefires squealed as the prickly plants groped them.

"Everybody happy?" asked Brigitta. The plants ignored her and continued nuzzling. Brigitta returned to the lyllium blossoms and searched for odorless flowers. When she had collected a dozen of them, she tied them together with twine and tip-toed out of the garden.

*   *   *

Hoping she had collected everything Hrathgar Good needed, Brigitta rushed through the passageway toward the dungeon. She stopped when she spotted Himalette trembling up against the stone wall grasping a metal bowl.

She moved silently to her sister and wrenched the bowl from her grip. Water from the cavern wall trickled down Himalette's back, soaking her clothes. She stood there shivering as her terrified eyes told Brigitta not to make a sound.

Brigitta's skin froze when she heard the cackling voice of Hrathgar Evil. "All these seasons, you have been working so hard for me, helping to perfect my stone spell ingredients with your fine gardening skills." There was the sound of metal clanking against metal as Hrathgar Evil traveled the length of her dungeon, rapping on the bars. "Even so, I still could not penetrate the White Forest's protective field, let alone leave our castle grounds, due to those filthy Elders' curse on us!"

"So you managed to enter the forest by hypnotizing one of their kin!" exclaimed Hrathgar Good. "You had that poor sprite perform your terrible magic from the inside!"

"What luck that I caught her spying on us!" Hrathgar Evil was positively giddy. "We have had so few visitors. And now it seems that our young Water Faeries have been touched by Blue Spell. What a delightful surprise!" She gave a maniacal laugh. "I'll split them open to find its magic!"

Himalette looked down at her blue arms and then back up at Brigitta, who wrapped herself around Himalette to keep her from shivering.

"You mustn't! They are only children!"

"Children who possess the secret of the greatest faerie magic! They will be mine, for when the Hourglass of Protection runs out at night's end, its hold on us will be relinquished. We will be two . . . and you will still be behind those bars."

"Then I will kill myself before the moons leave the sky," said Hrathgar Good bitterly, "so that you will die along with me."

A large bone-dweller scuttled by, its tail brushing against Himalette's leg. Brigitta covered her sister's mouth with one hand to keep her from crying out.

"In your position, I find that highly unlikely."

They heard Hrathgar Evil shuffle away and then the clank as she shut the front bars of the prison. When they were sure Hrathgar Evil was out of hearing range, Brigitta and Himalette poked their heads into the dungeon. Himalette gasped. A stone Minq sat in front of Hrathgar Good's cell with wide frozen eyes and mouth.

"Minq!" Himalette ran over and hugged him.

"You do not know how sorry I am." Hrathgar Good's face hung with sadness.

"We'll turn him back, Himmy, I promise."

"And she wants to take our blue!" wailed Himalette.

"We won't let her, do you hear?" Brigitta handed Himalette the metal bowl. "Quickly now, go fill this bowl with water from the passageway walls."

"That's what I was doing when Hrathgar Evil—"

"It's okay, Himmy, she won't come back. She'll be looking for us someplace else." Brigitta turned to Hrathgar Good. She removed the blossoms and the spell-seed and placed them on the floor in front of the cell. She retrieved the Eyes from behind a rock.

"I forgot to warn you about the prickly munshmins," said Hrathgar as she rolled up her sleeves. "They are a noisy bunch, but they remember everything. Ask a munshmin, I always say." Hrathgar Good reached carefully through the bars for the flowers and spell-seed. "They did not give you any trouble?"

"Not at all," said Brigitta, smiling to herself.

Brigitta, Himalette and Hrathgar stared at the metal bowl filled with the lyllium nectar potion. The submerged Eyes didn't look any more alert. Himalette bent down on her hands and knees for a closer look.

"It's not working," she said.

"It has to work." Brigitta examined the bowl.

"You are certain he said lyllium blossom nectar, not pollen or essence?" asked Hrathgar in a faraway voice.

"Yes, yes." Brigitta stood up and paced back and forth.

"If this plan does not work, I have another." Hrathgar picked up the spell-seed.

"What's in it?" Brigitta asked.

"A gardener's weapon. An extremely poisonous root tincture."

"We'll poison Hrathgar Evil?"

"I am sure you could not get close enough to give it to her." Hrathgar placed the spell-seed on the ground and spun it three times. "No, no . . . I will poison myself."

"What?" gasped Himalette.

"If I do so before night's end, Hrathgar Evil will die along with me."

"No!" Himalette cried. "You can't!"

"This will work," Brigitta said, kneeling back down to look at the Eyes. She gave the bowl a little shake.

"Brigitta, even if the Eyes do resuscitate, how will you ever get them past the Evil One to view her spell book?" Hrathgar Good looked at the girls tenderly. "I am sorry to have made you an accomplice, Brigitta, but it is my choice."

She wiped a tear from her cheek.

"That was your plan all along, wasn't it? When you sent me for the lyllium and asked me to get the spell-seed?" Brigitta looked at Hrathgar in disbelief.

"You are a wise faerie." Hrathgar dabbed the tear on the top of the spell-seed. Then dabbed a second one.

"No, no! We won't let you," Himalette cried in despair.

Hrathgar Good looked intently at Brigitta and gestured toward Himalette. "I know you understand."

Himalette shook her head back and forth, tears streaming down her face, "No, no, please!"

"Unfortunately," Hrathgar said, lifting her finger and placing the third tear on the spell-seed, "if the Evil One is destroyed, you might never be able to break the stone curse." The spell seed crackled in Hrathgar's hands. "But at least we will have saved your faerie kin from being ruled by a monster. It is the very least I can do for all the suffering I have caused."

The Eyes twitched in the bowl. Brigitta and Himalette let out a simultaneous cry as the Eyes rose unsteadily into the air and shook themselves off. Momentarily distracted, Hrathgar paused long enough for Brigitta to snatch the spell-seed, burning both her arms as she pulled it out of Hrathgar's reach.

The Eyes fluttered about the room and bounced against the far wall, then turned around and flew back. Himalette jumped in front of them, waving frantically. "Gola!" she called happily. The Eyes blinked at Himalette several times and bobbed in the air.

When the Eyes turned and saw the stone Minq, they looked back at Brigitta and Himalette with concern. They continued examining the room, approaching Hrathgar and hovering in the air to get a good look at her face.

"Hello, Gola." Hrathgar blinked back at the Eyes. "It has been a long time."

"The necklace!" Brigitta exclaimed. She set the spell-seed down and pulled the mirrored locket from inside her tunic to see Hrathgar's face reflected back at her. She smiled. "Gola will see."

"Yes, but I fear the next step is nearly impossible." Hrathgar looked away from the Eyes and stared at the spell-seed on the floor.

"And we haven't much time," Brigitta realized, tucking the mirrored necklace back into her tunic. She tapped her wings together.

Hrathgar paced in her cell. "We must think of a way to distract the Evil One so you can get to her book."

"Briggy?" Himalette asked.

"I could use myself as a distraction," Brigitta suggested.

"Too dangerous."

"Briggy!" Himalette called.

"In a moment, Himmy . . ."

Himalette folded her arms in front of her chest and gave an exaggerated sigh.

"Yes, Himalette?" Hrathgar stopped pacing and looked at the young faerie.

"Hrathgar Evil said she hypnotized the sprite using green zynthias."

Hrathgar Good turned to Brigitta in wide-eyed wonder. "I see cleverness runs in your family."

● ● ●

Clicking her two stones together in a slow rhythm, Brigitta lead the way past the sleeping rock guards.

"I hate rock dragons," muttered Himalette, twisting the gardener's bag in her hands.

"Shhh," hushed Brigitta. She nodded to the Eyes to lead the way and when they were out of rock dragon reach, she pulled out her mirror necklace. She sent the Eyes up and over the wall of the castle. She and Himalette peered into the mirror as the Eyes made their way to the courtyard and settled behind a bush. Brigitta and Himalette flew up over the side.

They immediately hid themselves under the bush and spied on the frogs. Most of the frogs were still gathered around the slain frog on the other side of the courtyard looking puzzled by its lack of movement. None of the frogs were guarding the entrance to the cavern below the castle.

"You stay here," Brigitta instructed the Eyes. "I don't want to fetch you out of another frog belly."

The Eyes bobbed in agreement.

Brigitta and Himalette hunted around under the bush and gathered as many stones as Brigitta could carry in the sack, remembering that they would need to save two in order to keep the rock dragons away. They streaked toward the cave entrance as close to the ground as possible and zoomed inside. They were immediately enveloped in the darkness, but it was easy enough to follow the crack in the earth. In a few moments the green glow of the zynthias appeared beneath them.

They emerged from the earth and looked away from the crystals, hovering high above the fierce river. Brigitta reached inside the sack and drew out several stones. She handed the sack to Himalette. "Whatever you do—"

"I know, I know, don't look at the crystals." Himalette flew below Brigitta and steadied herself. She opened the sack, turned her face away and squeezed her eyes shut. "Ready!" she hollered.

Facing the opposite direction, Brigitta blindly threw one of the stones toward the crystals. It bounced off the ceiling and plummeted to the river. She threw a second stone and missed again. She adjusted her position and threw a third stone, knocking several crystals from the ceiling.

"Did you catch any?" shouted Brigitta over the roar of the river.

"No. Do it again!" yelled Himalette.

"Move farther to your right."

Himalette followed the instructions, squeezed her eyes tighter and opened the bag. Brigitta took a deep breath and threw a fourth stone. Crystals came raining down from the ceiling.

"I got some! I got some!" Himalette said gleefully. "I can feel them in my sack!"

"Let's try again, just in case," said Brigitta, "and Himmy?"

"What?"

"You're doing great."

When they were sure they had more than enough zynthias in the bag, they returned to the cold crack in the earth and made their way back up the crevasse. Just before they reached the opening, Brigitta felt around in the bag, gathered a few crystals, and launched them into the courtyard. Himalette giggled and Brigitta hushed her. They waited a little while, then emerged from the tunnel to find four hypnotized frogs gathered around the zynthias.

Brigitta and Himalette muffled their laughter as they flew back to the waiting Eyes. The Eyes looked at them quizzically from under the bush.

"I wonder why the Eyes aren't hypnotized by the crystals?" Himalette said.

Brigitta shrugged, pointed to her own head, then pointed to the Eyes. "No brains?"

The Eyes blinked back at them. Brigitta gestured to the courtyard wall, and the Eyes turned and made their way back down the side of the castle.

Brigitta handed the sack to Himalette. "Can you carry that all right?"

Himalette nodded confidently. Brigitta picked up her two lullaby stones and they slipped over the wall.

Chapter Nineteen

Hrathgar Good was astounded when Brigitta held up the bulging sack of green zynthias. "Well," she said as they maneuvered the sack through the prison bars, "you two are full of surprises."

Brigitta pulled her hand away, grazing her fingers on the hot metal. She blew on her fingers to cool the sting.

"You're sure this will work?" she asked Hrathgar.

"We are connected, two as one." Hrathgar Good pulled up her sleeve, revealing a long scar. "This is where Hrathgar Evil burned herself several moons ago."

"Will we be able to unhypnotize you afterwards?" asked Himalette suddenly.

"It does not matter." Hrathgar rolled down her sleeve and gripped the sack tightly. "Brigitta, remember, if this does not work, if Gola cannot undo the curse, you must promise to give me the poison before night's end."

"No!" pronounced Himalette, checking to see that the spell-seed was well out of Hrathgar's reach.

Brigitta, too, glanced at the spell-seed leaning up against a rock, then over to the stone Minq. "I can't . . ."

"I am old. Think of your sister." She dropped her

voice, "Brigitta, the Evil One would do anything to find the secret of Blue Spell. And she is most unsympathetic."

Brigitta nodded and fluttered to Himalette. She looked into her troubled eyes and took her hand. "Gola will see."

Hrathgar Good wrapped the edges of the sack tightly around her wrists and gripped it so hard her fingers turned white. "I hope so, my faeries, for all our sakes." She opened the sack and looked inside. Her eyes glazed over as the zynthia hypnosis set in.

⬥ ⬥ ⬥

Brigitta and Himalette hid outside the doorway of Hrathgar's spell chamber. Brigitta sent the Eyes into the room and peered into her mirror necklace.

Himalette craned her neck to look. "Did it work?"

Brigitta lowered the mirror so Himalette could see the image of Hrathgar Evil's ugly frozen face. They smirked at each other and entered the chambers. The Eyes hovered in front of Hrathgar Evil, who stood perfectly still in the center of the room. The Eyes fluttered about her face, bumped up against her forehead a few times, then gave a satisfied nod.

Brigitta and Himalette slowly approached Hrathgar and studied her immobile form. She wasn't frozen like the stone faeries, all lifeless and gray. Her wrinkled yellow hands looked as if they might dart, fingernails first, to one of their throats at any moment. Brigitta's eyes were drawn to the moonstone around her neck, but she caught herself before she could be pulled into its mind-distorting darkness.

Brigitta tugged on her sister. "Careful, Himmy, not too close."

Himalette stuck her tongue out at Hrathgar as Brigitta turned her attention to the spell book, open on the podium.

"How will we know if Gola can read it?" asked Himalette as they dashed across the room.

"We'll just have to hope she can." Brigitta turned the book to the first page and looked at the foreign forest language. She whistled softly for the Eyes. The Eyes slapped Hrathgar upside the head with a wing before making their way over to the spell book. "Okay, do your thing," said Brigitta, pointing to the page.

The Eyes puffed themselves up as if taking a deep breath, then proceeded to scan each page as quickly and thoroughly as possible, pausing every so often to study something further. Brigitta turned the pages as the Eyes scanned. Himalette pulled up a stool to watch. The only sound in the room was the quiet flick of each page.

🍂 🍂 🍂

Brigitta and the Eyes had a good rhythm going. She turned the pages and the Eyes scanned each line and then nodded when they were ready for the next page. The Eyes began to wobble, dizzy from the movement. Brigitta gave them words of encouragement.

She flipped another page. "Good work! More than half-way now."

Himalette got down from her stool and stretched

her arms and wings. She wandered around the room, glaring at Hrathgar Evil. Suddenly Himalette gasped and flew back to Brigitta.

"Brigitta, she moved! I saw her move!"

Brigitta whirled around and studied Hrathgar Evil, who remained still. "It's all right," she said, and turned back around, flipping the page quickly.

"Hurry, Briggy, hurry!" Himalette yanked on Brigitta's tunic.

The Eyes picked up their pace, but exhaustion was setting in. They were bloodshot, their lids drooped, and their wings fluttered erratically. Himalette approached the book and fingered the remaining pages. "Almost done," she breathed.

"Interesting reading?" a chilling voice inquired from behind them.

Brigitta, Himalette, and the Eyes whirled around in terror. Hrathgar Evil rubbed her hands together and stretched her limbs. A wicked smile broke out across her sallow face.

The Eyes turned back to the book and started scanning in double-time. They turned the pages with their own wings and kept scanning. Brigitta and Himalette fell away as Hrathgar Evil stormed over to the book and knocked the Eyes aside. They slammed into the wall, dropped to the floor, and lay there motionless.

Brigitta and Himalette flew to the door. Hrathgar picked up a round, dark green object from her shelf and hurled it across the room. It landed in front of them and grew rapidly into a thorny vine, blocking the doorway.

The girls backed away from the plant as it grew and grew, stretching out toward them with menacing speed.

Brigitta held her sister and they trembled together, caught between Hrathgar and the twisting vines, which lashed out and grabbed them by the ankles. The girls shrieked as the vines crawled up their legs and squeezed them in a thorny hug.

"Nice try," growled Hrathgar.

• • •

Hrathgar Evil pushed Brigitta and Himalette into the dungeon. Chained to each other by the ankles, they lost their balance and fell to the cold stone floor. They looked over as Hrathgar Good groaned from her cell. She picked herself up and shook herself awake. Underneath her lay the bag of green zynthias. She steadied herself, and then leaned over to pick up the bag.

"Do not think of it, dear sister." Hrathgar Evil yanked the girls up and thrust them toward Hrathgar Good's cell. She reached her gnarled hand around Himalette's throat.

Hrathgar Good looked into Himalette's desperate eyes. She looked back down at the bag of zynthias. "The bag—it must have slipped from my grasp."

Hrathgar Evil snapped her fingers. A small bone-dweller scurried across the floor and into Hrathgar Good's cell where it nabbed the bag of zynthias in its teeth and dragged it out between the bars. It squeaked as the bars singed its fur, and the acrid smell of burning bone-dweller hair filled the air.

"I am afraid the night is coming to an end," the Evil One said. "In a few moon-beats, your forest will be completely unprotected." She dug her nails into Brigitta's shoulder and leaned closer to the frightened faeries. "The Center Realm will make a lovely stone garden. I will line your Council of Elders around your precious Hourglass and your High Priest will guard my front door."

Brigitta yanked herself from Hrathgar Evil's grip. "You'll never even touch High *Priestess* Ondelle!"

"Ondelle!" Both Hrathgars turned to Brigitta.

Hrathgar Evil's grip loosened around Himalette's neck. Himalette turned and kicked at Hrathgar's ankles. Hrathgar knocked both girls to the ground.

"That traitor Ondelle of Grioth is now High Priestess? Ha! Even better! I will enjoy eating my breakfast while I gaze upon her sorry stone face." She picked up the ends of the heavy chain and pulled the faerie girls across the floor. "Now, how would you like to watch as my sister's forgotten body is consumed by bone-dwellers?"

She shoved Brigitta and Himalette toward the next cell with a rough kick. She laughed and lifted her leg again. Himalette cowered, but Brigitta looked up at Hrathgar defiantly, until the empty space in front of Hrathgar Good's cell caught her attention.

"Where's Minq?"

"What?" Hrathgar Evil whipped around.

Himalette looked out from behind her hands and Hrathgar Good began to chuckle.

Hrathgar Evil picked up the two faeries by the hair and dragged them back to Hrathgar Good's cell as

160

they shrieked in pain. "What did you do with him?" she demanded. "Where is he?"

"I did nothing," responded Hrathgar Good.

"Gola did it!" cried Himalette.

"She read the book and broke your curse!" snarled Brigitta at Hrathgar Evil.

"No!" Hrathgar Evil lost her grip on the girls' hair and they dropped to the ground. "No. Impossible."

Like a lightning bolt, Minq sprang from the tunnel and headed for Hrathgar Evil, teeth bared. He leapt into the air and slammed a spiky stone into the back of Hrathgar Evil's head. Both Hrathgars cried out and grasped their skulls. Both pulled their bloody hands back and stared at the thick red liquid in shock.

Hrathgar Evil whirled around and smacked Minq solidly with her arm. He fell against the cell bars, crying out as they burned into his back. Hrathgar Evil swiped the spiky stone from the ground, picked Minq up by the ears, and held the weapon to his face. She glared down at the frightened faeries huddled together on the floor. "You will all suffer greatly for this."

Himalette cried hysterically. "Please, no!"

The Evil One lifted the stone and stared into Minq's dazed eyes. "The little faerie will be next."

Brigitta looked frantically from her little sister to Hrathgar Good, then back to her sister. "I don't think so!" Brigitta grabbed Himalette's hand and with all the strength she could muster took a flying leap, chains and all, landing next to the spell-seed.

Hrathgar Evil spun around. Brigitta snatched the

open spell-seed from the ground. Hrathgar Good reached through the bars, scorching her arms. Hrathgar Evil gasped as her flesh was burned and she dropped Minq from her powerful grasp.

Brigitta hesitated.

"You must. She will kill you all!" Hrathgar Good pleaded, reaching farther, baring the pain as gray-green smoke drifted from her burning arms.

Hrathgar Evil screamed and lunged toward Himalette.

"No!" Himalette shrieked and jumped backwards.

Brigitta tossed the spell-seed to Hrathgar Good's waiting hands. In one swift motion, she pulled it to her lips and downed the poison.

Hrathgar Evil took one more heavy step toward them, then wobbled slightly on her feet. Regaining her balance, she zigzagged across the floor and reached for the bars of Good Hrathgar's cell. Her hands sizzled as she started to choke. Both Hrathgars clutched at their throats and fell to the ground.

Brigitta, Himalette, and Minq rushed to the cell. Brigitta reached through the bars, ignoring the burn, to take Hrathgar Good's hand. Hrathgar coughed and smiled.

"Isn't there anything we can do?" pleaded Brigitta. "A potion? A spell?"

"No, our suns and moons are over," Hrathgar smiled weakly.

Himalette held onto Brigitta. Minq wrapped his ears around them both.

"Please, tell the Elders that I am so very sorry for our

transgressions." Hrathgar squeezed Brigitta's hand. "But I hope now, at least, I have made amends for them."

"I will tell them how kind you were," Brigitta managed to say through her tears. "How brave."

"And tell Ondelle of Grioth . . . " Hrathgar closed her eyes, "I am so pleased to have finally met you."

Hrathgar's grip loosened from Brigitta's hand, and before she could ask Hrathgar what she had meant, both Hrathgars coughed a few more times and then were still. Brigitta, Himalette, and Minq stared at the two Hrathgars in silence.

The moonstone amulet around Hrathgar Evil's neck began to glow. Minq pulled the girls back with his ears. They watched as the white-blue light grew brighter and warmer.

"No look," commanded Minq, shading the sisters' eyes with his ears.

As the light reached them, Brigitta began to tingle, as if being enveloped in thousands of miniature stars. The sensation spread from the outside of her body inwards until she felt her whole being would burst with joy. Himalette laughed next to her. Brigitta took her hand.

Then the warmth and tingling receded and Minq removed his ears from around their eyes.

There was only one Hrathgar lying on the ground outside of the cell.

Brigitta kneeled in front of her. Hrathgar's skin was soft and rosy and her eyes were crystal white. Her mustard wings were spread beneath her, and in a deeper shade, the destiny markings of an Elder colored the tips of each: eyes with four radiating lines in four directions.

Himalette crawled to Brigitta's side and peered into Hrathgar's face. "Her eyes! What happened to them?"

"The Ethereals," said Brigitta, closing Hrathgar's eyelids, "they have dispersed her energy."

"They were here? They came back?"

"Yes, they came back." Brigitta wiped Himalette's soiled blue nose with her finger. She pulled it back and examined her blue hand, wondering if the Ethereals had been protecting them all along.

Brigitta reached over and gently kissed Hrathgar's cheek. "Thank you," she whispered. She removed the moonstone amulet from Hrathgar's neck and handed it to Minq.

Minq gave a little bow to Brigitta and accepted it. He picked up the open spell-seed and placed the amulet inside. The spell-seed made a little kissing sound as it sealed itself up again.

Chapter Twenty

Hearts torn from their loss, Brigitta, Himalette, and Minq dragged their weary bodies up the castle stairs and through several passageways until they found themselves in the courtyard. Four hypnotized frogs sat around the zynthias. The rest were perched on top of the shortest stone wall, staring out over the forest. As the trio tentatively entered the courtyard, the frogs glanced at them, then turned their attention back to the forest. They went on ignoring them as Brigitta took a few steps toward the wall.

Brigitta shrugged. "I guess it's okay now."

"We should help those ones," said Himalette, pointing to the hypnotized beasts.

Unfurling his great ears, Minq picked up the zynthias with them and scrolled the crystals up inside. The four frogs wobbled a bit and then collapsed. "They okay." Minq examined them. "Be in shock."

He trotted over to the crack in the earth and peered into the great darkness that led down to The River That Runs Backwards. He lifted his ear to drop them inside.

"Wait!" Brigitta fluttered over to Minq. "Better save one just in case. Might come in handy someday."

Minq dropped all the zynthias save one into the crevasse. Brigitta looked at her torn tunic and laughed. "I'm all out of sleeves."

Himalette ripped one of her own sleeves off and handed it to Brigitta, who wrapped the zynthia inside. As she slid it into her pocket, Himalette squealed and pointed over the wall. "Briggy, look!"

In the far distance, a shimmering blue light cut through the dark air.

"It's coming from the White Forest!" Brigitta cried, and without thinking, ran the rest of the way to the wall. She stood between two frogs, who looked down at her indifferently.

"Hooray!" cheered Himalette, pulling Minq to the wall with her.

As the three travelers watched, the blue light grew brighter and brighter.

"What mean?" asked Minq.

"They've reset the hourglass," said Brigitta, beaming down at her sister. "Everyone is safe. We can go home."

The blue light rose from the darkness and slowly faded to mist. The mist floated up into the sky and disappeared into the night.

"That's my favorite part of the ceremony," said Brigitta, "when the mist disappears. I used to think the Ancients lived among the stars."

"I like the singing and dancing best," said Himalette.

"Of course you do," teased Brigitta.

After the light show had completely faded, the frogs turned toward Brigitta, Himalette, and Minq. Brigitta quickly counted twelve of them, plus four more dizzy frogs in the courtyard.

"Uh-oh," Minq said under his breath.

Suddenly, one of the frogs hopped from the wall, landed on the other side, and blinked several times as if seeing the world for the first time. Another frog followed, then another and another, until they were all hopping down the mountain.

"I guess their mean spell was broken," said Brigitta, putting her arm around Himalette.

"I still hate frogs," muttered Himalette, waving good-bye to them as they hopped away. When the last frog had leapt from the wall, even the four dizzy ones, Brigitta, Minq, and Himalette turned back toward the castle. A small shape fluttered out of one of the windows.

"Gola's Eyes!" whooped Minq, holding out his free ear.

The Eyes wobbled about as they examined Minq's offered ear, then they fumbled toward Brigitta. She held out her arm and they landed on it, staring into Brigitta's face, and blinking in weary pleasure.

"Thank you, Gola," Brigitta said. She pulled out the mirror necklace and held it up. Her own smiling face shone back at her.

Himalette craned her neck to look into the mirror. Brigitta scratched her nose. A layer of grime came off, revealing her blue skin underneath.

"Hey," said Himalette, suddenly getting itchy herself. She scratched her right shoulder. "We're still blue."

"Yeah," Brigitta said as she poked Himalette in the

stomach playfully. "But I bet there's someone back home who can fix it."

Without Hrathgar Evil's presence, the castle now only exuded an ancient sadness as if it knew it had once been beautiful. Brigitta, Himalette, and Minq trudged in silence back down through the castle and retrieved Hrathgar's body. They carried it to her garden and laid it to rest next to the lylliums, covering it with soil and blossoms. The munshmins and gwenefires were silent out of respect for the faerie who had nurtured them.

When Hrathgar's body was concealed and they had each said a few words of gratitude, Brigitta turned and stared down at the prickly plants. "Ask a munshmin," she murmured to herself.

"What!" they growled.

"How do we get down the mountain through the poison clouds?"

"Hmmmmm . . . heh-heh-heh," laughed the munshmins.

Brigitta was in no mood to be teased. She lifted her foot above the munshmins as if to stomp on them, but they only howled with laughter. "Tell me!" Brigitta commanded.

The gwenefires shook their leaves at the munshmins and they grumbled amongst themselves until the gwenefires turned their flower faces away and folded their leaves.

"Fine, fine, fine," chattered the munshmins, thrusting their bulbs forward. "Delia grass. Chew, chew, chew it.

Delia grass." They gestured toward a patch of grass, then turned and tickled the gwenefires. "And breathe through your mouth. Yes, breathe through your mouth."

Brigitta plucked a handful of sticky green grass and handed some to Himalette and Minq. They each popped a blade into their mouths, and then immediately spat it back out. "It's awful!" Brigitta grimaced.

The munshmins nearly split their stalks laughing. Minq growled back at the flowers as he and the faeries left the garden. As worn out as they were, Brigitta and Himalette couldn't help giggling themselves. They stuffed flower petals in their noses, placed the delia blades back in their mouths, and chewed.

With two rocks each, they descended the mountain, taking turns banging out a lullaby to keep the rock dragons at bay. Brigitta was too tired to fly, and too tired to speak, but there was a lightness within her. She knew the Hourglass had been turned and that her momma and poppa, Auntie Ferna, and High Priestess Ondelle were safe.

As the day broke and scattered morning sunlight through the valley below, they continued as if sleepwalking, barely conscious. Nothing could penetrate Brigitta's haze. Even the wild sound of The River That Runs Backwards was like a distant dream. She put one foot in front of the other, again and again. She knew Himalette must be exhausted, but her little sister didn't complain, not once the entire way down the mountain. Not even when Minq and Brigitta had to pull thorns from her arm or when she tangled herself up in a vine.

The sun was leaving the sky again by the time they

reached Gola's tree. Brigitta thought they would all surely collapse before they could get inside. Gola stood in the doorway, looking down at them with her empty eye sockets, a pair of Eyes on each shoulder. Brigitta stumbled into her and hugged her strange barky body, which smelled of earth and moss. Gola hesitated for a moment, then wrapped her arms around Brigitta in return.

"It is time to rest," Gola said, and led them inside.

Brigitta sat up with a start and looked around. She was in Gola's bed. She heard a familiar laugh and caught sight of Himalette in the kitchen, stirring a pot under Gola's supervision. Several pairs of bored Eyes watched as the spoon went around and around.

Minq burst through the door with an earful of firewood and noticed Brigitta on the bed. "You wake!" He dropped the wood and trotted to Brigitta. "Help you down. Sleep long time."

Himalette gave an excited squeal and Brigitta didn't even cringe. "We're going home! We're going home! And Minq and Gola are coming with us!"

Minq gave a shy smile as Gola shuffled into the room. It was so hard to read any expression on her ancient face, but Brigitta sensed that she was smiling, so she smiled back.

"Yes, Himmy, yes." Brigitta hugged her sister. "But first, I'm hungry! Is there anything to eat?"

Gola laughed. "Your sister has made you a healing stew."

Brigitta ate four bowls of Himalette's stew before her hunger was satisfied. As their momma and poppa would be very worried, they decided they would leave the following morning, and spent the rest of the day helping Gola gather her belongings and replant her flowers in the forest.

No longer suspicious of her every move, Brigitta watched Gola shuffling about her tree home. She was older and more feeble than Brigitta had realized. Her clothes were horribly tattered, which made Brigitta feel sorry for her. She thought perhaps a White Forest faerie could make her a new tunic, something warm and soft against her jagged skin.

Gola was also one of few words, carefully chosen. Brigitta imagined it was the effect of many moons of solitude and suspicion. There was something about her way that made Brigitta respect that silence. Himalette, however, chatted on enough for the both of them about birds and caterpillars and grovens and, of course, their momma and poppa. Brigitta thought Gola showed magnificent restraint in not knocking Himalette on the head with a spoon.

After Gola had packed her books, she took the ancient map down from the wall. Behind it was a spell seed. She brought it to Brigitta. "Your zynthia. Safe for traveling."

Gola's moonstone shone from around her neck. It was even more beautiful than Brigitta had remembered. She noticed tiny cracks in the stone, among the stars, that she hadn't seen before.

"The moonstone," she said, "it's not affecting my mind any more."

"It is where it is meant to be."

As she watched Gola roll up her map for the trip,

Brigitta couldn't hold back her questions any longer. "Gola, your map, where did it come from?"

"Long ago, I received it as a gift from one of your Ancients." Gola placed the map into a beast skin and tied it.

"But . . . " Brigitta was astonished. "That means . . . before the Great World Cry?"

"Shortly thereafter," said Gola, placing the map with her growing pile of personal items.

"How can that be?" asked Brigitta. "You must be . . . I mean you're . . . "

"Very old." Gola patted Brigitta on her head.

Brigitta wanted to ask Gola so many more questions, like what the Ethereals had been like and how she met them. She wanted to know what Faweh had been like before the Great World Cry. But then she thought about Hrathgar, and how her pursuit of knowledge had ended badly. Gola was wise, and must have kept information back for a reason.

Maybe, Brigitta thought, knowing too much before one is ready can be a bad thing. Like having strong wings or access to potion magic before you knew what to do with them.

"Aren't you going to miss your tree?" asked Himalette, interrupting Brigitta's thoughts. She sat by the pool brushing her blue-tinted hair, clean and shiny from a recent wash.

"It was my destiny to live here," said Gola, "and now it is my destiny to leave."

Gola, Minq, and the faerie sisters stood in front of Gola's tree with packs lashed to their backs. Gola had a small wheeled box for her heavy books and jars. They watched as Gola's Eyes flew from the windows in a jagged black stream and fluttered about excitedly. Himalette danced around them in the air.

"The Eyes are flying home with us," sang Himalette as they made their way across the field of whisper lights. *"The Eyes are flying home."*

A dozen flowers shivered as they passed, releasing their centers. They began to glow, first white, then yellow. As the whisper lights drifted around their heads. Brigitta heard their shiny voices in her ears.

"They're laughing," said Himalette, "Right, Briggy?"

"Yes, they're laughing." Brigitta raced across the field, releasing more flower centers, laughing along with them.

Chapter Twenty-One

Even with Gola, Minq, and all the Eyes along for the journey, the Dark Forest was still a frightening place, and Brigitta couldn't wait to get home as soon as possible. Gola may have had every magical item she owned with them, but she was no match for a giant caterpillar. She was slow, and her Eyes were sometimes temperamental and lazy. Brigitta noted how much concentration it took for Gola to walk, although she was pretty handy with her cane, which was so strong it could practically lift her over fallen logs.

They spent the first night in a shallow cave. Brigitta thought it was a good spot, until Gola woke them before the sun had risen to tell them they must leave immediately before the vicious occupant of the cave returned for his daylight sleep.

The second night they spent in the rock fortress Minq had taken them to after they had escaped the caterpillar. It seemed like seasons ago, Brigitta mused as they entered, then smiled, realizing they would be home by the next moonsrise.

Minq and Himalette snuggled together by the fire and were fast asleep before the first log burned. Brigitta sat next to Gola and stared at the row of sleepy Eyes perched on a rock. She counted them a few times and was sure there were less pairs of Eyes than when they had started.

"Gola, your Eyes!" She craned her neck to search the shadows. "I think some are missing."

"Yes," responded Gola, looking wearily into the fire.

"What happened? Where are they?"

"There have been predators along the way."

Brigitta realized why Gola's concentration had been so fierce as they had journeyed through the forest. It wasn't just because of her elderly limbs; she had been using the Eyes to keep the danger away. She could see danger coming through her Eyes and even lure it from them.

"Thank you," murmured Brigitta, then she shuddered. She felt terrible about Gola sacrificing her Eyes for them. They were not just her creations, they were her companions. "And thank you for reading Hrathgar's book and lifting the curse on the White Forest. Thank you for saving my momma and poppa."

"I did not lift the curse on your forest," said Gola. "I could only lift the curse on Minq because he is my familiar. The rest was your doing."

"What do you mean?"

"I am not versed in faerie magic. I could not undo a curse cast from within your own forest any more than I could undo the spell that protected you from that curse." Gola poked at the fire with her cane. "It was Hrathgar's death that undid the curse."

"I didn't mean to . . . I didn't want to . . ." Brigitta lay her head down in Gola's lap. There were no words for how sorry she was for her part in Hrathgar Good's demise. She began to cry, softly at first, and then in great heaving sobs.

"It was your destiny." Gola stroked Brigitta's face with her long, jagged fingers. "What is done is done."

* * *

Brigitta, Himalette, Gola, and Minq stumbled out of the Dark Forest into The Shift. Gola had seen the way through her Eyes, but until Brigitta could touch the earth on the other side of the protective field, she wouldn't feel safe.

As soon as they saw that wide expanse of bare land, Brigitta and Himalette cried with joy. As they crossed The Shift and jettisoned through the watery field, they were met by an Air Faerie male with long teal wings and an Air Faerie female with translucent lavender ones. They both had three darker bands on the ends of their wings, the destiny markings of White Forest Perimeter Guards.

Brigitta explained to the Air Faeries that Gola and Minq had saved their lives, but the Air Faeries seemed to know this already. She noticed that the guards shuddered as they passed through the field toward Gola and Minq. No faerie, not even a Perimeter Guard, likes to be outside the White Forest, she thought.

"You have to go with them," Brigitta called to Gola and Minq. "It's the only way for you to cross."

The Perimeter Guards escorted Gola and Minq across The Shift. The female Air Faerie sped ahead to bring the news of their arrival, and the rest of the party made its way to the Center Realm.

Pippet's shrieks filled the air as she zipped toward her daughters, nearly knocking them over with the force of her embrace. Mousha followed as quickly as his small wings could carry him and together they cried tears of relief and joy, thoroughly examining their strange blue children. After rubbing at their skin in disbelief, they exclaimed at each bump, bruise, and cut they found. Brigitta and Himalette swore again and again that they were fine as they kissed their parents' faces.

"But your skin!" exclaimed Pippet.

Remembering that they still itched, Brigitta and Himalette both began to scratch.

"I rather like it," said Mousha. "No one else has ever had blue daughters!"

Faeries swarmed them, fussing and asking questions. Minq and Gola shied away, not used to so much attention. The younger faeries were fascinated by Gola's Eyes and tried to play with them. Brigitta had to shoo the children away for fear of Gola getting dizzy from their over-excitement.

As more and more faeries crowded around them, Minq knocked over a table, catapulting pipberry pies and tingermint teacakes into the crowd. The whole celebration was far too overwhelming for Brigitta, and she guessed for her sister as well, so she grabbed Himalette's hand and they escaped during the commotion. They hid themselves behind a large uul tree to wait for the official ceremony marking their return.

177

They watched as Mousha led Minq into the festival grounds to view the new inventions, and Ondelle took Gola into The Hive, the Elder chambers, to speak with her privately. Although Brigitta was tempted to spy on them through the secret passageway, that would mean leaving the safety of the tree, and Brigitta wanted to be left alone until the last possible moment.

Several moon-beats later, Ondelle and Gola returned, and all of the faeries from each of the four realms assembled in the festival fairgrounds. Flowers of every color imaginable fell from the trees and dancing shadowflies pulled bright streams of paper through the air. Cheering faeries packed the stands, and Pippet, Mousha, and Auntie Ferna grinned proudly from the front row of the Water Realm seats. To Brigitta's great relief, wearing an immense leafy bandage on his arm, Orl Featherkind sat to Pippet's right. Edl Featherkind sat next to him, applauding.

The Elders sat down in their council chairs in front of the steps that led to the great Hourglass. Brigitta, Himalette, Minq, and Gola were guided up the steps of the silver platform by four Elder Apprentices, a male and female from the Water Realm and a male and female from the Earth Realm, bearing shimmering hourglasses encircled by the four elemental symbols on their silver tunics.

Brigitta and Himalette held hands and gazed up at the Hourglass, smiling as the colored sands trickled silently through the narrow crystal tube. High Priestess Ondelle made her way across the platform to the four guests of honor and stared down at Brigitta and Himalette who scratched her nose nervously as Brigitta squeezed her hand.

Ondelle quieted the cheers and applause with a wave of her scepter and addressed Gola. "Gola, for your generous assistance, if you so desire, I invite you to live with us in our protected land, partaking in all our customs. As well, we would be honored to have you serve as an advisor to our Council of Elders."

A pair of Eyes hovered in front of Ondelle's face. They gave an awkward bow and flew away again. "Thank you," Gola said solemnly as the Eyes landed on her shoulder and surveyed the crowd. "I would like that very much."

Ondelle's amused gaze landed on Minq. The High Priestess motioned to the two male Elder Apprentices and they flew onto the stage carrying a glass box with a pair of translucent wings inside.

"Minq, for risking your life to save our beloved kin, I present you with your own faerie wings."

She waved her scepter and the two faerie men opened the delicate box and held up the wings. Minq gazed at them, too stunned to speak. At Ondelle's urging, he slipped into them and grinned in his strange toothy way. Ondelle pointed her scepter at him, a stream of colored beams spilled out over the wings, and they began to flap. Minq tested them a few times, then flew up, knocking into the two faerie men, who nearly dropped the glass box.

"They may take a bit of getting used to," Ondelle pointed out as Minq landed with a sheepish smile.

"And Minq can stay, too?" asked Himalette.

"And Minq can stay, too," said Ondelle as Minq took off once again, bumping into her and knocking her scepter from her hand. The audience tittered as she gave him an unconvincing frown and picked it up.

She moved in front of Himalette and held out her hand. One of the female Elder Apprentices placed a necklace in her palm, which she fastened around Himalette's neck. It held a glowing, disc-shaped amulet.

"Himalette, for your quick thinking, aiding your sister in saving our dear home, I present you with the element of fire, which will serve you well on your next grand adventure."

"I'm a Fire Faerie now?" Himalette examined the disc excitedly.

Ondelle laughed. "Not exactly."

Himalette considered this. "That's okay . . . it's not so bad being a Water Faerie." Himalette beamed up at Brigitta. "But I'd like to keep it all the same. It's pretty."

Ondelle gestured to the second female Apprentice who brought her a clear shallow dish of sparkling liquid. She dipped her hands in the liquid, then turned and caressed Himalette's face with them. Himalette's face turned back to its regular pinkish hue and the color spread through her body and out across her wings. Himalette gave a loud sigh of relief and the crowd burst into laughter.

Ondelle leaned down and gave Himalette a hug. Himalette blushed and looked out at her momma and poppa as they wiped proud tears from their cheeks.

Ondelle then moved to Brigitta. Her black eyes turned serious. Brigitta held her breath as her heart pounded in her chest.

"Brigitta of Tiragarrow, for bravery under extreme circumstances, I present you with our highest honor, Protector of the Forest."

The crowd sat in stunned silence as Ondelle removed her own hourglass necklace from around her neck and placed it over Brigitta's head.

The Elders gasped. Air Elder Fozk of Fhorsa stood up from his chair. "Ondelle!" he cautioned.

"This necklace contains sands charged with each of the four elements," continued Ondelle, ignoring Fozk's outburst. Fozk sat back down and the Elders whispered amongst themselves.

Ondelle slipped her hands into the shallow dish once again, closing her eyes as they soaked in the liquid. "With time, you will learn how to cultivate its power." She opened her eyes, turned to Brigitta, and paused.

Their eyes connected. Brigitta felt a rush of anticipation.

Ondelle reached down and took Brigitta's face in her hands. Relief spread through her skin and she sighed as she watched the blue fade away from her arms. There was a collective gasp from the crowd and Brigitta looked up. She found her momma's and poppa's wide-eyed expressions in the front row. Pippet's hands darted to her open mouth.

Brigitta looked up at Ondelle. "What? What's wrong?"

"Nothing is wrong, my dear one," said Ondelle with a smile so beautiful it broke Brigitta's heart. "Look at your wings."

Brigitta craned her neck and stretched out her wings. Her mind went numb and her stomach lurched as she stared in awe. At the top of each velvety wing, in a stunning deep green, were the unmistakable markings of an Elder.

At the top of the Water Faerie grandstand, Brigitta sat alone, watching as all the White Forest faeries celebrated below. A pair of sprites played lively music on a glass flute made for two, accompanied by three Earth Faeries drumming on carved tree stumps. Air Faeries led games of cloud-tossing around dancing faerie couples. Festival decorators lit candle webs stretched across tree branches to carry the festivities into the evening.

Catching Brigitta's eye, Pippet waved between feverishly dishing out cups of iced frommafin to thirsty families. Brigitta sighed and waved back, then searched the festival grounds for the rest of her family. She watched as Mousha showed Minq how to use his new wings, Gola and Fernatta huddled together in deep discussion of who knows what, and Himalette chased pairs of Eyes around the trees with four other faerie children.

As Brigitta observed the festival activities, she felt distant and numb, like she was on the outside of something looking in. She noticed her three Water Faerie friends, with the markings of a Cooking Teacher, a Village-Nest Caretaker, and a Star Teller. They are so carefree, Brigitta thought as a young Fire Faerie boy zipped between two of them, tousling Dinnae's hair. Giggling like gwenefires, the trio dashed after him into the crowd.

Gwenefires, munshmins, rock dragons, Hrathgar Good and Evil . . . Brigitta shook her head, wanting to leave those images behind for a few suns, to pretend, for a short while, it had all been a bad dream. Her chest tingled where the miniature hourglass lay, and its warmth penetrated her skin, comforting her even though it spoke to her heart in a language she didn't understand.

"You are not going to join your friends?" Ondelle landed beside Brigitta and sat down.

"I don't know." Brigitta looked at all the cheerful faeries below. She felt small and awkward with Ondelle's powerful presence beside her.

"You are concerned with the markings on your wings."

"How can I not be?" Brigitta burst out, looking up into Ondelle's black moon eyes, holding back her tears. "It's got to be a mistake."

"Why would you think that?" Ondelle asked.

"I can't—I don't know how—I'm not qualified!"

"There is much to learn, of course. You will apprentice for many seasons."

"But Elders are so wise." Brigitta felt defeated. She would certainly be laughed at when everyone realized how completely wrong she was for this Life Task.

"Tell me," asked Ondelle gesturing out toward all the celebrating faeries, "what kind of faerie would think of traveling to Hrathgar's castle for assistance? And what kind of faerie would have taken on such a brave mission?"

"An Elder, I suppose." Brigitta sighed. "But we had to do something. We were desperate! And I wasn't marked as an Elder when I left the White Forest."

"Would your choice have been any different if you had known your markings?"

"I don't know." Brigitta was lost in confusion. "Was

I marked as an Elder because I saved the forest or did I save the forest because I was destined to be an Elder?"

"That sounds like the question of a very wise faerie."

🍃 🍃 🍃

Ondelle led Brigitta into the Elder chambers and pointed to the chair meant for the Water Faerie Elder, a post currently held by the jovial Jorris of Rioscrea. Brigitta nervously sat down in the plush seat of the high-backed chair and felt a rush of dizziness. Ondelle placed her hand on Brigitta's arm and the dizziness vanished.

"It is the previous Water Faerie Elders speaking to you all at once. It takes several seasons to learn how to separate their voices."

"It felt like a swarm of butterflies in my head."

Ondelle laughed and her dark eyes twinkled. Brigitta stared at them. They were so happy and so sad at the same time. She glanced across the room, through the entry way, at the wall where she and her friends had been hiding. Ondelle's gaze followed hers, but she said nothing.

Ondelle turned and sat down in her own chair and studied Brigitta for a moment before speaking again. "On the day the stone curse took our forest, I noticed our sprite, Vivilia, with the black spell-seed. Moments later, I noticed her again without the spell-seed. I was reminded of the night Hrathgar tried to steal the power of the Hourglass three hundred seasons ago." She leaned back in her chair. "She had used a similar seed."

"She stole that from Gola."

"Yes." Ondelle's eyes drifted away from Brigitta and back to the entrance of the chambers.

"Priestess Ondelle," said Brigitta quietly, "on that day, we were hiding . . . Did you know?"

"I sensed your presence."

"And later, the sprite came to us. She protected us. Did you know that, too?"

Ondelle stood again and slowly paced back and forth in front of her chair. "Brigitta, sometimes, as Elders, we possess information of which other faeries are not aware. For instance, Fernatta of Gyllenhale and I are the only remaining faeries who know what truly happened on the night Hrathgar attempted to steal the power of the Hourglass."

"All I know is that Gola's moonstone split Hrathgar in two."

"Yes, and I am afraid the rest of the Elders and I, as well as the High Priest of the time, had not the knowledge to return her to her single self. I am ashamed to admit that we hid both Hrathgars away and then conjured Blue Spell to imprison her in the ancient castle on Dead Mountain."

"Nobody else knew about the two Hrathgars?"

"It was too painful to admit that we were banishing Hrathgar Good, a faerie so dear and innocent. She herself agreed it was the only way to keep Hrathgar Evil from accessing the White Forest." Ondelle sat back down. "Mind you, this decision weighed heavily upon all of us. Particularly on Fernatta of Gyllenhale, who resigned as an Elder due to her sorrow."

"But, Auntie Ferna isn't an Elder. She has the

markings of a Chronicler."

"She was only an Elder for a few seasons before the incident. Most have forgotten as her markings have faded and only the inner circle of the eye glyph remains. Look closer and you will see."

"How can destiny markings change? Aren't we all marked for life?"

"Each one's destiny unfolds differently. Fernatta's markings changed because it was her destiny for them to change."

"Gola said it was her destiny to leave her home, but where would she have gone if we hadn't met her?"

"What do you know of a Drutan's moonstones?" asked Ondelle.

"I know they are bad for anyone except their rightful owner."

"A Drutan, a Tree Being, may receive several moonstones at birth. Each reveals a new path along her life. Without fulfilling them, she will never take her final root in the earth. She will decay instead, slowly and painfully."

Brigitta shivered at the thought.

"The moonstone Hrathgar stole contained her final destiny."

"What did it tell her?"

"That it was her destiny to help save the White Forest where she would spend her final days."

"That doesn't make any sense." Brigitta was more puzzled than ever. "What if Hrathgar hadn't stolen it? Then Gola's destiny wouldn't have been fulfilled!"

"And here is something else." Ondelle's eyes narrowed. "I was the one who sent our sprite to Hrathgar's castle. She was to report back to the Elders on Hrathgar's health and status. Does this mean I was the one who brought the curse upon our forest that served in fulfilling Gola's destiny?"

Brigitta shook her head. "Destiny is a confusing thing. I don't know if I'll ever understand it."

"One thing I have learned," said Ondelle, "is to allow all destinies to unfold as they should. This becomes challenging if one . . . " Ondelle glanced briefly toward the spot where Brigitta and her friends had been hiding, " . . . knows things that others do not."

Brigitta suddenly recalled Hrathgar's final words in the dungeon. "Hrathgar said something odd. She said to tell you she was glad to have finally met me."

Brigitta detected the faintest twitch in Ondelle's face, so faint she could almost convince herself it didn't happen.

"Yes, that is an odd thing to say."

She waited for Ondelle to elaborate, but when she didn't, Brigitta wasn't surprised. "It must be very lonely having to keep so many secrets," she said softly.

Ondelle only smiled. "Your mind is very busy, Brigitta. You will make a fine Elder some day."

Brigitta was doubtful but didn't argue with the High Priestess.

"Right now, however, there is a celebration to attend." Ondelle stood once more and gestured toward the chamber entrance. "It is time for you to remember that you are still a young faerie and not too old for games."

Three suns later, just after breakfast, Brigitta stepped into the lyllium meadow, followed by Pippet, Mousha, Gola, and Auntie Ferna. Tiny white flowers greeted them under a warm sun. Himalette zipped over their heads, followed by Minq on his unsteady wings.

"Lower to ground, Himalette!" Minq cried. "Lower to ground!"

Himalette dropped down closer to the ground and joined the others as they made their way to a simple memory-marking of interlocking silver tree branches. Set into the branches, bright yellow crystals spelled out: HRATHGAR THE GOOD. Brigitta placed a purple keronium glass below the branches. Himalette landed, stuck a few fragrant crotias in the glass, and took Brigitta's hand.

"I wish she could have returned," said Brigitta as she wiped a tear from her sister's cheek.

"We will forever be in her debt." Pippet put her arms around her daughters.

"Yes," Brigitta agreed, although her mind was busy replaying Ondelle's words. Destiny was so confusing. If Hrathgar hadn't cast the spell in the first place, her Evil half at least, there wouldn't have been anything to save. But still, deep in her heart, she knew that the Good Hrathgar was the real Hrathgar, and she was more than grateful for her sacrifice.

"She's not gone, you know." Mousha gestured outward. "She's simply merged with the elements. The Ancient Ones will look after her now, as they have always done."

Brigitta looked closely at her poppa's destiny markings, the brownish question marks, the symbols of an Inventor. She looked at her momma's wings, a beautiful dusty pink with swirls of darker pink dots marking her as a Feast Master.

Auntie Ferna kneeled down beside Hrathgar's memory-marking. Her eyes were moist despite her smile. Brigitta noticed that the dark circles on her ginger wings were outlined by very faint eye-shapes and two even fainter lines radiating up toward air and fire. Ondelle was right. Brigitta couldn't believe she hadn't noticed this before. She wondered what other details she had failed to perceive.

Gola's Eyes fluttered to the memory-marking, examining the keronium glass and the flowers. From out of the woods, a large orange butterfly flew past and the Eyes followed it. The butterfly flew around them a few times, then landed on the top of the silver branches. The Eyes landed next to it.

There was a small spitting sound and the butterfly transformed into the Center Realm's sprite. Brigitta put out her finger. The Sprite touched it and bowed delicately.

"Vivilia," Brigitta murmured. She was lovely to look at, Brigitta decided, and silently thanked her for being part of the destiny she still didn't understand.

"Can I touch her, too, Briggy?" asked Himalette, holding herself back with great restraint.

"Yes, lola, you can touch her, too."

As Himalette reached out, the sprite flew away, laughing. She returned to her butterfly form and crossed the meadow, with the Eyes fluttering after her.

Himalette pouted. Everyone else laughed. Brigitta reached down and hugged her little sister, wondering what destiny markings would appear on Himalette's wings when the time came.

White Forest Lexicon

Ancient Ones

Another name for the **Ethereal Faeries** (fifth element). They brought the **elemental faeries** north during the **Great World Cry** and created the protected realm known as the White Forest. They are the keepers of **Blue Spell**, the highest form of faerie magic. They are no longer visible in the physical realm, but do "visit" each elemental faerie on two occasions: to mark their destiny at birth and disperse their energy at death. They also impart knowledge to the new High Priest or Priestess upon confirmation. They believe an individual's destiny, as well as the planet's destiny, should unfold without further interference on their behalf. (see also **elemental faeries**)

beasts

Faerie term for all animals (there are flying beasts, buzzing beasts, swimming beasts, burrowing beasts, hopping beasts, etc.). Some faeries consider themselves to be beasts, others don't.

Blue Spell

The highest form of faerie magic, the secrets of which are passed down by the **Ethereals** (or **Ancient Ones**) to each High Priest or Priestess upon confirmation. The Ethereals used it to create the protected realm of the White Forest and "charge" the sands of the **Hourglass of Protection**. It is so powerful to the **elemental faeries** that it is reserved for rare and extreme circumstances. Only the High Priest or Priestess has the authority to conjure it, and only through consensus of the White Forest Elders, or by the approval of the Ethereals themselves. These precautionary measures were necessary after the tragedies of the **Great World Cry**.

bone-dwellers

A large rodent that lives off of dead flesh and bones. Somewhat blind and deaf, they are not very skittish. They are also not dangerous to living beasts, just ugly and foul-smelling, with long, wiry whiskers, bald pink heads and tails, and thick matted brown fur on the rest of their bodies. If any are around, there is something dead close by.

breath-lantern

An Air Faerie specialty made of wood and translucent fabric. Inside the lantern is a small cloud treated with a fire spell. When a faerie blows into it, the cloud glows bright orange. Quite beautiful and surprisingly sturdy.

candle webs

A very special decorative candle that is spun, just like a web. There is no wick. Any portion of it may be lit, including the entire web, which is often done during festive occasions.

carnivorous caterpillars

Caterpillars in the dark forests of **Foraglenn** can grow to be quite large and vicious. They cocoon other living animals and suffocate them. Their offspring (see **glow worms**) chew through the cocoons and eat the remains. Carnivorous caterpillars do not turn into butterflies.

NOTE: There are also ordinary caterpillars that turn into butterflies across **Foraglenn** (as well as on **Pariglenn** and **Storlglenn**). They are harmless distant cousins to the carnivorous kind. Carnivorous caterpillars do not eat regular caterpillars. They don't like the taste.

The Change

The Change is a time between childhood and adulthood, lasting several seasons. It is a time of introspection. Young faeries are moody during this time as they contemplate their Life's Task, which is revealed as a symbol on their wings that marks the "official" onset of their change. During this time their wings also grow longer and stronger, shedding once, twice, or sometimes three times and emerging brighter and more colorful. It is said by the adults that children wouldn't know what to do with such wings unless they had a purpose.

chatterbuds

One of Gola the Drutan's numerous creations. Her chatterbuds were created, more for pleasure than practicality, from a potion watered over them when they were seedlings. They grew up in the cauldrons lining her walkway, keeping her company with their friendly chatter. Gola prefers solitude, but she is wise enough to know that a being needs others to talk to in order to stay sane.

chroniclers

Earth Faeries have always been destiny-marked as chroniclers and they keep track of everything in books. Once a Chronicler disperses with the elements, her books are moved to the lower levels of **The Hive**. Any faerie may request access to these books, although very rarely do they bother. Faeries aren't known for being that interested in reading. Faerie Lorekeepers keep track of the history of the White Forest. Fernatta of Gyllenhale is the 8th Faerie Lorekeeper.

Continents of Araglenn, Carraiglenn, Pariglenn, and Storlglenn

(See **Foraglenn**)

crotia

A distinct plant with yellow-green leaves and extremely fragrant multi-colored petals. Used for perfumes, candles, oils, bath salts, and other pleasant smelling items. Has warming properties. Not recommended for eating as it would taste like perfume and might make one sick.

Dead Mountain

The castle on Dead Mountain is where Hrathgar was banished. Before the **Great World Cry**, when **Faweh** was balanced, and the five civilizations flourished together, the castle on the mountain was used as a retreat for the Sages and their guests. It was a sacred place. At that time the mountain was referred to as Dragon Mountain, and on a clear day one could see all the way down the continent to the mountains surrounding the **Valley of Noe**. (See **Lake Indago**.)

delia grass

Delia means faith. Delia was also the name of the High Sage from **Storlglenn** who created the grass before the **Great World Cry**. The only place it exists outside of Storlglenn is **Dead Mountain**, because she planted some in the castle garden while visiting there. The grass grows from a spell that allows the chewer of the grass to resist harm or to rapidly heal, but only if the chewer believes they will. It has no power if the chewer does not have faith in the magic of the grass.

deodyte

Faeries may procreate with faeries bound by other elements. As when giving birth to a boy or a girl, there is a dominant element. For instance, an earth faerie and a fire faerie may give birth to a fire girl, fire boy, earth girl, or earth boy. Once every great while, a **deodyte** will be born. This is a faerie of duel elements.

These faeries are respected, though slightly feared due to their enigmatic personalities. Their Life Tasks are usually something self-directed and less social.

dragon flower (or dragon egg flower)

The center of the enormous red and green flower is a speckled white bulb that looks like an egg in its mouth, so it is often referred to as a "dragon egg flower." Dragon flower grows sporadically in very wet areas. It takes the dew from four or five "eggs" to fill even the smallest **keronium glass**. It is used as a binding and activating agent in potions.

Drutan

A "Tree Being." There are several scattered about the continent of **Foraglenn**. They live a very long time (longer than faeries) and are solitary beings. They have faerie-like body features (such as hands, fingers, arms, toes, knees, ears, etc.) except that they are much taller and their skin grows progressively more fibrous and bark-like as they age and lose their facial features. They are quite good with magic, especially dealing with plants. When they die, and if they have properly fulfilled their destiny, they simply stop where they are and take root, almost indistinguishable from the actual trees. (see also **moonstones**)

elemental faeries

The faeries of the White Forest are bound by one of four elements: earth, air, fire, water. This affects their appearance (i.e. skin and hair tone, body shape), talents, and temperament. Faeries tend to live in the realm associated with their element, but there is no law that keeps them there and many faeries find mates of another element. For the most part faeries celebrate, respect, and appreciate each other's differences. Although they sometimes become impatient when dealing with each other, they are happy to allow other elemental faeries to do the tasks they aren't interested in, which keeps everything in balance. (see also **Ancient Ones**)

Eternal Dragon (Tzajeek)

When the Elders work spells, they call forth the power of the Eternal Dragon, Tzajeek, a sea serpent with the ability to absorb elements. Instead of a fire-breather you might say it's a fire-*eater* ... and an earth, water, and air eater. It is Faweh's true Keeper of the Elements and the only one of its kind. Its origin is unknown.

Before a High Priest or Priestess takes position, he or she must journey, alone, to the Sea of Tzajeek to receive private wisdom from the Eternal Dragon. When the faeries lived in the Valley of Noe, Tzajeek would appear in Lake Indago to counsel with the High Sage once every season cycle. But after the **Great World Cry**, Tzajeek became a traveler of the open seas.

Most elemental faeries only think of Tzajeek as a mythical creature from ancient tales.

Ethereal Faeries
(see **Ancient Ones**)

The Eyes

Gola, a gifted **Drutan**, developed a special breed of eyes with wings that can see for her. Drutans are not known for their eyesight and as they grow older, their own eyes sink further and further into their barky skin until they disappear completely. Gola's Eyes allow her to continue to see in her old age. She also has a shallow pool in the center of the floor of her home that allows others to see what her Eyes see.

Faweh

The planet is called many things by many beings, but the White Forest faeries simply refer to the outer world beyond the White Forest as Faweh, which literally translates to "house of elements."

feather paints

Feather paints are used on the decorative feathers of festival costumes. The thin and delicate paint is specially made to coat feathers. It dries very fast, so one can dip the feathers in multiple colors. Fire Faeries are expert feather paint makers and are extremely competitive when it comes to making the best paint. The colors are seemingly endless and the most popular are the sparkled and metallic versions.

Festival of Elements

Faeries love festivals. They love singing and dancing and eating and games. The Festival of Elements is the most important festival in the White Forest due to the rotating of the **Hourglass of Protection**. The Ethereals designed the White Forest so that it would be protected against incident or intruder by the magic of the Hourglass, which contains sands empowered by **Blue Spell**. As a preventative measure, however, the sands' Blue Spell power runs out every **season cycle** to prevent any possible evil-minded being or intruder from having access to too much power. (see also **Blue Spell** and **Hourglass of Protection**)

flutterscarves

Scarves created primarily for dance and entertainment. They are so light and airy they can be directed by even the slightest breeze. They jump about in the air if a faerie so much as waves her hand past them.

Foraglenn

Beyond the White Forest, the elemental faeries have mapped very little. They have a general idea of the continent upon which they live and the four smaller continents beyond. They refer to their continent, the largest, as **Foraglenn**, and the other continents (in order of size): **Pariglenn**, **Araglenn**, **Carraiglenn**, and **Storlglenn**. Each continent has its own distinct geography, history, flora, fauna, myths, and magic. There are no other known faerie realms on the other continents, although there are rumors and mythic tales of renegade faeries who wander these lands.

frogs (giant)

In addition to a variety of regular-sized frogs, there are giant frogs on the continents of **Foraglenn**, **Pariglenn**, and **Storlglenn**, but they are fairly harmless. They are also not the smartest hopping beasts in the forest. They do eat small flying beasts, but faeries are generally not on their menu. Hrathgar Evil's frogs were cast with a spell to be especially aggressive.

frommalin

A bubbly refreshment served iced or hot. Usually reserved for festive occasions as it takes a long time to prepare. Made with **tingermint** and **pipberries**.

globelight

A faerie's flashlight. Not difficult to make, but tricky to make well. If one has a good mold and can read a cookbook, one can make a globelight. However, it takes a skilled faerie to make one that stays charged for any length of time. Globelights are round, fit in the palm of one's hand, and give off light from any part that is rubbed. Use a thumb to make a spotlight, swipe the whole thing and hang it for a night dance.

glow worms

Glow worms are the offspring of **carnivorous caterpillars.** When young, they feed on the flesh of beasts cocooned by the caterpillars. They lose their glow after eight to ten suns, then enter an extraordinary growth spurt, after which they are able to make cocoons of their own. They are quite vulnerable in the between time, however, and are susceptible to the elements and predators. Most never make it to their full size. When they die, they are also cocooned and eaten.

goldenfew

A very traditional festival stew made from fermented **gundle-beans.** Sort of like lentil soup for faeries, but more tangy. It warms one up inside when eaten. It is not uncommon for various forest creatures to gather around the bases of village trees during festival preparation, hoping for an inferior batch to be discarded. Buzzing beasts are particularly fond of goldenfew as it makes them tipsy.

Great Moon

The larger and bluer of the two moons of **Faweh.** It travels across the sky more slowly than the smaller moon. Sometimes referred to as the Great Blue Moon or just Blue Moon.

Great World Cry

A pivotal moment in Faweh's history, when the energies that kept the planet peaceful and balanced collapsed. This happened when the World Sages misused the power of **Blue Spell** and the High Sage (one of the **Ancient Ones**) was killed. They threw his body into **Lake Indago,** a sacred lake that was the source of all the elements. The lake dried up and out sprung **The River That Runs Backwards,** a symbol of the chaos of energetic forces now inhabiting the planet.

green zynthias
A crystal with hypnotic properties, very common inside the caves beneath **Dead Mountain**. Also found in caves in many parts of the continent of **Araglenn** (one of plenty of reasons not to visit).

grovens
A furry purple toad-like creature with very large eyes and fat lips. They are slow and not very bright. Sometimes faerie children keep them as pets, but they aren't very exciting. They aren't sad, but their expressions might lead one to believe they are. Playing with them is harmless, but it's best not to follow them home, as they live in a slimy bog filled with **stench-mold**, where they gather to mate, give birth, and raise their young. They spend the rest of their time wandering around the forest, eating creepy-crawly beasts and sleeping in damp places. They have no sense of smell and poor eyesight, but their hearing is pretty good.

gundlebeans
A hearty, extremely versatile faerie staple. "Eat your gundlebeans" is probably the most common phrase out of a mother faerie's mouth at the dinner table. Plump, meaty brown beans that grow in great clumps on vines all over the White Forest. One can eat them straight off the vine or cooked in a variety of dishes such as pie or stew.

gwenefire
Used for love potions, hypnotic potions, dream potions, and seduction potions. Long lavender and pink flowers with lashes. Very fragrant. Very potent.

The Hive
The Hive is what the White Forest faeries fondly call the Elders' enclave underground in the Center Realm. It consists of spell

chambers, living quarters for Elders and Apprentices, libraries, storage for all sorts of magical items, and access to many of the underground passageways of the forest.

Hourglass of Protection

An enormous hourglass located in the Center Realm of the White Forest shaped from the branches of two immense **uul trees** and inlaid with transparent crystal that only the **Ethereals** know how to form. Its protective magic (see **Blue Spell**) keeps the forest safe from the outside world. Once every **season cycle**, during the **Festival of Elements**, the hourglass is turned, the elemental sands are rebalanced during a sacred ritual, and the protective shield is renewed. Only the acting High Priest or Priestess has the knowledge to rotate the Hourglass, and can only do so with the assistance of at least two White Forest Elders.

keronium glass

A very delicate hand-blown instrument used for measuring ingredients for potions and spells. Each glass must be blown to perfection and have the right amount of element. The sizes from smallest to largest are: yellow, orange, red, turquoise, and purple. There are 20 different kinds of keronium glassware (i.e. earth orange, fire orange, water orange, etc.)

Lake Indago

Many, many seasons ago there were several sophisticated civilizations on **Faweh**. There was also a very large faerie population, centered in the Valley of Noe, in the southern region of **Foraglenn**. The valley housed a great quantity of faerie villages, which are now in ruins, many completely vanished forever. These villages peppered the shores of the enormous Lake Indago, the former source of all elements, which now births **The River that Runs Backwards** into this world.

licotia nectar

Licotia nectar is really only used to make nasty tasting potions go down better. It comes from a deep purple flower that grows in the tops of the trees only in the White Forest. It's challenging to gather not only due to the height at which it grows, but because the nectar bulbs are slippery and difficult to remove. Luckily, it only takes a few drops to flavor a potion as it is very strong and no faerie would ever drink it without diluting it first. Also used in a soothing faerie treat called "triple lyllium suclaid."

Lola Moon

The smaller, oranger of **Faweh**'s two moons. Lola means "small one" or "little one." Sometimes older sisters call their little sisters "lola" or parents use it as a term of endearment. Also referred to as Sister Moon, especially in faerie lullabies.

lyllium

Non-descript, leafy plant with delicate white flowers. Inside each flower is a small nectar pouch. Lyllium is used for its restorative properties. It isn't capable of bringing a full-sized beast back to life, but it could cheer it up if it were unhappy. The nectar must be drained and needs to be prepared for use in potions. Eating the flower alone has very little effect. The flowers are quite fragrant when they first bloom and as they lose their scent, the nectar becomes more potent.

Minq

Minq is a pale brown, hairless cross between a fox and rodent with exceptionally long and useful ears, which he uses like a spare set of front legs. He latches on to others for safety, pledging allegiance if necessary. He has never met another of his kind. Many **Drutans** have animal "familiars" and Minq is Gola's. If a forest beast accidentally devours a piece of a Drutan's rooted parent, mistaking them for a tree, destiny draws them together and the connection is understood at once. Gola rescued Minq from a large bird when he was a young pup and he has been with her ever since, although she is not possessive and encourages his independence.

moon-beat

A way of measuring the passing of time using the traveling speed of the **Great Moon**. One moon-beat is approximately 15 minutes. The smaller **Lola Moon** travels faster than the Great Moon, so that it always appears to be chasing it, or running from it, across the sky. If a faerie is in a hurry, one might say to her, "What's your rush, Lola Moon?"

moonstone

A **Drutan**'s most prized possession. Drutans are always born at night. When a female Drutan is ready to give birth, she passes the baby through her bark-skin to a pouch in the male. The male "plants" the baby in an open area under the moonslight and then continues on. The mother, father, and child might never see each other ever again. When the child awakens, its first tears, mingled with the two moons' light, form moonstones, which the Drutan will use for the rest of his or her life. Each stone is unique and reveals a portion of the Drutan's destiny. Moonstones formed under two moons are more powerful than when formed under one moon. A Drutan born under no moon light receives no moonstones and therefore perishes quickly. Moonstones are particular to their owners and have mind-altering effects on others who attempt to use them: they become separated from rational thought and suffer from a division of personalities.

munshmins

Extremely annoying, precocious, and loud-mouthed plant. Dark purple, thorny, with large-lipped bulbs. They make great burglar alarms and are also used in potions that involve making inanimate objects speak. They have an excellent genetic memory, and can often remember information overheard many seasons in the past. Although they don't ever share information unless they feel like it, they are not known to lie.

pipberries

Named after the small "pip" sound they make when a ripe one is poked and breaks open, spilling its delicious juice. The riper they are, the sweeter they taste. They are so tempting that when they start to get plump and red it takes a very disciplined faerie to wait for them to fully ripen.

Precipice Waterfall

The largest waterfall in the White Forest, located southwest of the Water Realm. **Spring River** (which begins northeast of the Earth Realm) ends at Precipice Waterfall, where the water runs over numerous rocks and crags and falls back into the earth and through a series of caverns running the length of the White Forest, leaving it lush and fertile. When the **Ethereals** first moved the lesser (**elemental**) faeries to the White Forest, several Earth Faeries charted maps of the caverns. The books are kept deep in **The Hive**'s library and most faeries have forgotten about them. Young faeries are not allowed into the caverns, and very few adult faeries have bothered to venture there.

pond vile

A nasty, carnivorous plant that lives at the bottom of some fresh water pools in the Dark Forest that don't get enough moonslight. It's easy to be fooled by the innocent looking little green feathery plants, but they can snag a beast quickly and pull it underwater with their little bulbs, which open up into barbed fingers.

River That Runs Backwards
(see **Great World Cry**)

rock dragons
Leftover beasts from an ancient time. Usually pretty lazy unless provoked, and being woken up from one of their numerous naps will provoke them. They only live in the vicinity of the castle at **Dead Mountain** (previously **Dragon Mountain**, since that's where the rock dragons lived). The ancient Sages had conjured them up to keep curious beasts away from the castle. There are about two dozen of them left. They do not procreate.

sand petals
Another measuring tool, like **keronium glass**. Sand petals are just that, petals made from crystallized sand. They aren't real petals from plants, it's simply a shape faeries are fond of that makes for a good spoon-like tool. They come in ½, full, and double sizes.

season cycle
There are three seasons: Grow Months, Green Months, Gray Months. Generally things are planted in the Grow Months, inventions are revealed, new recipes tried, new songs and dances shared. During the Green Months, there is a lot of activity and each village-nest and elemental realm hosts festivals and community events. The Gray Months are a time of learning, studying, harvesting, and developing new feats, inventions, recipes, songs, and other projects. Instruments are built for songmaking in the Gray Months. The Elders work on their spells. It is a more serious time . . . although most faeries don't stay serious for long.

shadowfly

Shadowflies are quiet flying beasts that perform patterned dances in the sunlight in order to communicate. Lots of faerie children daydream while watching them as they are quite mesmerizing. If a faerie studies the shadows long enough, they can figure out what the shadowflies are saying. The messages are usually reports about the weather or where certain flowers are in bloom.

sharmock roots

A common ingredient in a variety of faerie stews, herbal medicines and spells. They are extremely versatile and pleasant enough tasting on their own (raw or cooked). The roots are bright orange and round, but they are difficult to spot on the forest floor because the top of the root looks like a common moss. However, they usually grow in large clumps, like crabgrass, so when a faerie finds one, she just pulls and she's in business. They grow well in the White Forest due to its particular balance of water and light. They are much less common in the Dark Forest.

The Shift

A moat of earth that stretches around the perimeter of the White Forest, keeping it separated and safe from the rest of the world. Through the middle of The Shift is a force-field that no one but White Forest residents may cross. Anyone who does not belong in the White Forest must be escorted across by a Perimeter Guard.

spell-seed

Another specialty of Gola the **Drutan**. Used for transporting potions or magical items. It is large, hard, wrinkled, and black and when closed it is vacuum-sealed and nearly impossible to penetrate. It is easily opened, however, by spinning it three times in the same direction the sun and moons travel, then balancing it on end and releasing three drops of water on it. It is odorless.

Spring River

Spring River is quite unique as it begins and ends in the White Forest. It bubbles from the ground in the Earth Faerie Realm, where is runs slow and wide. It narrows as it heads south west through the Water Faerie Realm, where it ends at **Precipice Falls** and is swallowed back into the earth through an endless series of underground caverns. This intricate web of catacombs distributes the water throughout the forest, making it extremely fertile land.

sprites

Sprites have been peripheral companions to the faeries for thousands of seasons. They were also brought to the White Forest by the **Ancient Ones** after the **Great World Cry.** They are much smaller, less communal, are not bound by an element, and have no destiny markings on their wings. They have a variety of skin and hair tones, but a uniform body type. There is no such thing as a chubby sprite. They are temperamental, prone to playing tricks on the elemental faeries, and consider themselves to be superior beings. They live in the **uul trees** surrounding the Center Realm, but mostly keep out of sight. There is always one designated as the Center Realm Sprite and he or she is a liaison to the White Forest Elders.

Star Teller

Star Tellers can tell what time of year it is by looking at the night sky. They keep track of the names of stars and create stories about them. They are often called to parties to tell Star Tales, which they do with great enthusiasm. The names of the stars and their stories tend to change, because not many Star Tellers bother to read old star charts. They prefer to make up their own, although there are a few favorite stories that have been passed down for several generations.

stench-mold

Not a fun thing for a faerie to get into. It's a slimy mold that smells like rotting eggs and is very difficult to get off. The only beasts it doesn't bother are **grovens**. It glides right off their slick fur. Grovens also lack a sense of smell.

thunder-bug

Thunder-bugs cling to branches and shake their back ends to make rhythmic, percussive sounds. They each have their own rhythm, so a swarm of them can be quite dizzying. When thunder-bugs are drunk on discarded **goldenfew** or lazy on **lyllium nectar,** faerie children like to catch them and put them in jars.

tingermint

A dusty-lavender flower that has a nectar used for flavoring. The nectar is earthy and sweet, with a tiny spicy zing when it hits the tongue.

uul tree

An ancient tree that oozes a light flavorless sap used for making spreadable tinctures or pastes. A very sturdy tree due to its thick trunk and twisting branches, which grow toward and into other uul trees creating canopies for young faeries to play in. Uul trees have been known to aid other trees by supporting them if they are in danger of falling or by oozing sap over injured bark. The Center Realm is surrounded by uul trees and the **Hourglass of Protection** is hung from the interlocking branches of the two largest ones.

Water Gardeners

Water Gardeners are Water Faeries who primarily work and live in the Earth Realm. They collaborate with the Earth Faerie gardeners to create marsh farms for plants that thrive in a wet environment. Earth Faeries tend to be good with plants and Water Faerie Gardeners are good at empathing (faerie sensing) the needs of water flora. Earth Faeries are also talented reed boat builders, which are used to tend the marsh farm crops.

weather spell

Faeries can't control the weather, but Water Faeries are quite in tune with it and can train themselves to empath (sense) clouds. Not only can they tell if it's going to rain, but if they are really good they can tell what kind of rain, how hard, or how big the drops will be. They can also train themselves to direct the wind. Weather spells can be used to encourage impending rain to come faster, slower, harder, softer, or even change the color of the drops (a favorite weather spell activity).

whisper light

The seed of the whisper grass, carried off by the breeze. The "whisps" glow yellow, which indicates they are ready to plant themselves. If the light is extinguished before it manages to plant itself in the ground the seed loses its fertility. Not only does a whisper light emit light, it also emits sound. The sounds are whispers, hence the name. Although it doesn't actually say anything that makes sense, it can drive one crazy trying to figure out what it is saying, because it sounds like *something*. In addition, what one hears them whispering is entirely a reflection of what's going on in one's own mind.

The Ruins of Noe

When faerie dead will not leave their bones
And babes maintain their eyes of white
When tongues of Elders start to moan
So a stranger will be caught in flight
And she who calls the stranger friend
who knows it by its name and kin
will travel back to times of old
and make the balance right again.

The balance of the White Forest has been disturbed and the Elders have lost contact with the Ethereals. Against their advice, High Priestess Ondelle asks Brigitta to accompany her to the old faerie ruins of Noe to find a way to reconnect with the Ancients.

What they discover when they arrive is something they never learned from any faerie tale. Why had this dark secret been kept from them? Why in the name of Faweh had the Ancients left some faeries behind?

Danika Dinsmore has been working and playing with children of all ages for 20 years. She is a poet, screenwriter, performance artist, and educator. She currently lives in Vancouver, British Columbia with her husband and their big-boned kitty Victor Gato.

Faerie Tales from the White Forest is her first novel series.

You can find *Brigitta of the White Forest* on Facebook or at www.thewhiteforest.com.